LOR...
WHERE ARE YOU?

DATE DUE

#47-0108 Peel Off Pressure Sensitive

YEARLING BOOKS/YOUNG YEARLINGS/YEARLING CLASSICS are designed especially to entertain and enlighten young people. Patricia Reilly Giff, consultant to this series, received the bachelor's degree from Marymount College. She holds the master's degree in history from St. John's University, and a Professional Diploma in Reading from Hofstra University. She was a teacher and reading consultant for many years, and is the author of numerous books for young readers.

LORETTA P. SWEENY, WHERE ARE YOU?

PATRICIA REILLY GIFF

Illustrated by ANTHONY KRAMER

68902

A YEARLING BOOK

Published by
Dell Publishing
a division of
Bantam Doubleday Dell Publishing Group, Inc.
666 Fifth Avenue
New York, New York 10103

The trademark Yearling® is registered in the U.S. Patent and Trademark Office.

The trademark Dell® is registered in the U.S. Patent and Trademark Office.

ISBN: 0-440-44926-X

Reprinted by arrangement with Delacorte Press

Printed in the United States of America

One Previous Edition

March 1990

10 9 8 7 6 5 4 3

CWO

For
Winifred and Bill Clark
with love

LORETTA P. SWEENY, WHERE ARE YOU?

DATE: July 1. Wed.
TIME: Early in morn.

V*A*C*A*T*I*O*N

Things to do this smmr:
1.   Find crime. (Mrdr if possible.)
2.   Solve.
3.   Finish reading Garcia's detective book.

**Name too plain. (Change when 16 if mother lets.)
Try diffrnt ones in meantime.

Françoise Floriot
(Maybe a French name)

CHAPTER 1

Abby poked her head out of the bedroom window. It was sunny and steamy hot outside. The street was filled with people.

She threw on her robe and went into the hall.

"Abby, is that you?" her mother called from the kitchen.

"Be right there," Abby said, her hand on the phone. "I just want to see if Potsie's up yet."

"I'll tell you what's up," her mother said, coming to the doorway. "The telephone bill." She dried her hands on a towel.

"It's Dan," Abby said. "He's on the phone every two minutes."

She took her hand off the phone and went into the kitchen. Her older brother Dan was at the table, hunched over a bowl of Honeycombs.

Abby slid into a chair. "I hope you saved some of that for me. It's my favorite kind."

He pushed the cereal box across the table. "I don't use the phone half as much as you do," he said. He looked up at his mother. "She's on the phone with Potsie more than she's off."

"Great," her mother said. "Daddy and I are killing ourselves working at the used car lot so you can have a phone marathon with Potsie."

Abby shook some cereal into her bowl. "At least I'm talking to a live person. Dan's always calling dial-a-joke, laughing, and carrying on. . . ." She broke off. "Hey. Where's the milk?"

Dan slid out of his seat. "None left."

"What do you mean . . . none left?" Abby asked. "What good is all this cereal without milk?"

Her mother looked at Dan. "Maybe you could run down to the deli."

He shook his head. "I'm going to try out for a job at the beach with Kevin Delio. Something up on the boardwalk. We've got to get there before the rest of the kids."

"What about your other job?" Abby asked. "Poop cleaner at the pet store."

Dan wiped his mouth. "Great for the winter. Not so hot for the summer." He laughed. "Get it? Hot. Summer." He hit Abby on top of her head, ducked around her, and disappeared down the hall.

"Dummy," she shouted. "Keep your hands off me."

"Stop dialing jokes," his mother called after him. "And you too, Abby. Stay off the phone." She poured a cup of coffee and looked down at it, frowning. "No milk."

4

"What about my cereal?" Abby asked. "I can't eat it this way."

"Daddy will be finished shaving in a few minutes," her mother said. "He'll want cereal, too. Be a good kid and go down to the deli. Get a half gallon."

Abby sighed and stood up. "All right."

Back in her room, she pulled on her shorts and the I SOLVE CRIME shirt that Potsie had given her for her birthday, and tucked her red memo pad into her back pocket.

Her mother was waiting for her in the hall. "Here's the money," she said. "And a bunch of raisins so you won't starve to death on the way."

"Thanks." Abby stuffed a few in her mouth and pulled open the door.

"Don't lose the money," her mother said. "Remember, a half gallon. And hurry. Daddy and I want to get down to the lot."

"Don't worry."

In the corridor, she checked the little arrow above the elevator doors. The elevator was up on the fifth floor. It would take forever to get down to two. It was so old that one day the ropes would probably break and the whole mess would crash into the basement.

She hoped she was there to see it.

She shoved the last of the raisins into her mouth and opened the door to the stairs.

Just in front of her on the landing was a wallet. It was purple with an orange streak of lightning across the middle.

She bent down and scooped it up.

———

Then, on the stairs below her, she heard the sound of footsteps. She leaned over the railing. For a moment, she saw a hand touch the railing below — a hand wearing a large ring that flashed glints of red and purple light.

Before she could call out, the outside door on the first floor opened and slammed shut.

She tore down the stairs, turned at the landing, and pushed open the door to the street.

There were about a million people scurrying back and forth.

She looked both ways, then darted around the garbage cans and raced down the street. It was so hot, she could feel her shirt sticking to her back.

She gave up at the corner. Leaning against the telephone pole, she yanked at the tab of the wallet and flipped it open.

"Loretta P. Sweeny," she muttered. "No address."

She reached into one of the pockets and pulled out a small piece of pink paper.

She stared at it, eyes widening. "Kill?" she whispered. "Kill?"

She shoved the paper back into the wallet. She'd have to get over to Potsie's. Right away.

She dodged around a parked car and headed across the street.

CHAPTER 2

Outside Potsie's apartment door, Abby leaned on the buzzer until she heard shuffling noises inside.

Potsie's mother, eyes half-open, unlocked the door. "Abby," she said. "I might have known." She pushed at her hair.

"Sorry," Abby said. "Is Potsie up? Can I wake her?"

"Be my guest," Mrs. Torres said. "Why should anyone sleep when I'm awake?" Barefoot, she padded into the kitchen. "On my day off, too," she groaned.

Abby rushed down the hall to Potsie's room and peered in the open door.

Potsie was rolled up in a lump in her pink canopied bed. She was sucking her thumb.

"Wake up," Abby said. "Right away."

Potsie opened her eyes and took her thumb out of her mouth.

"I thought you said you'd rather have your thumb cut off than . . ." Abby began.

Potsie held her thumb up in the air and closed her eyes. "I have no willpower. Come back in an hour. Come back tomorrow. I'm sleeping late."

"Never mind about that now," Abby said. She shoved a pile of underwear off a green bean bag chair and sank down on it. "It's the first day of vacation and I have a mystery to solve. Wait till you hear."

Potsie rolled out of bed and slid down to the floor. "I don't want to hear about any mystery. All I want to hear about is the beach. And the water." She rubbed her eyes. "I'm dying of the heat."

"Are you listening?" Abby pulled the wallet out of her pocket and held it up. "Some girl lost this on the stairs."

"Purple and orange," Potsie said. "Freaky. Who'd carry a wallet like that?"

"A murderer, that's who."

Potsie rolled her eyes. "Where does she live? Far away, I hope. Mail the wallet back. Tell her good luck, happy hunting. Then get your bathing suit. You promised me all winter you'd learn to swim."

"Swim? Are you crazy?" Abby pulled out the paper. "Just listen to this:

EVERYONE FEELS SORRY FOR CINDY.
BUT I WILL PROBABLY HAVE TO KILL
HER ON THE 4TH OF JULY. (I MUST WATCH
P. VERY CAREFULLY.)"

" 'P.' " Potsie squeaked. " 'P.' Does she mean . . ."

"Don't be silly," Abby said. "She doesn't even know you. At least I don't think . . ." Her voice trailed off.

"We've got a killer on our hands, Pots. Ready to strike. I knew it. The minute I saw that wallet lying on the stairs. It had that look somehow. Dangerous . . . mysterious."

Potsie was staring at her. "Take it down to the police. To Garcia. Right away."

"Wait a minute," Abby said. "Plenty of time. Remember this is only Wednesday . . . July first. Let's see what else is in here."

She fished through the pockets. "Look at these teeny little rubber bands. They just about fit on top of my pinkie."

"I don't want to look," Potsie said. "I don't even want to think about . . ."

Abby shook her head. "This is exciting, Pots. A real mystery." She held up one of the rubber bands and stared at it. "Maybe she's a midget and she has teeny little midget ponytails."

"Not so funny, Abby."

"Here's something else." Abby held up a stack of small red cardboard cards:

SISTER AMELIA
AND HER GRANDDAUGHTER
PRINCESS RITA ROSE
UNVEIL THE MISTS OF THE FUTURE

They looked at each other.

"The fortune-tellers at the beach," Potsie said. "I remember from last year."

Abby closed her eyes. "Come one, come all. Five dollars will reveal the future."

9

"And a dollar will give you a hint," Potsie said.

"That's a terrific clue," Abby said. "We'll have to get right down to Sister Amelia's. . . ."

"I'm going swimming."

"You're always afraid," Abby said. "You can't stand danger. . . ." She broke off and began again. "Don't you see, Potsie? We can go to the beach. In fact, we have to go to the beach. We'll start with the fortune-teller. . . ."

Potsie pulled her hair off the back of her neck. "On one condition."

"I know — that I learn to swim. Sure I will. As soon as I have a chance. Maybe in a couple of —"

"Today. Otherwise I'm not going near that fortune-teller's booth."

Abby hesitated. She thought about the dark blue water, and the waves reaching out. She shuddered. "Maybe. All right. I guess so."

She stood up. "I'm going home for my knapsack. I'll meet you at the bus stop."

DATE: Still Wed.
TIME: Later in morn.

CASE #2

(Case #1 was HAVE YOU SEEN HYACINTH MA-
CAW?)

Garcia's book says: KEEP A CAREFUL LIST OF EVI-
DENCE.

List of evidence:
1. Killer's wallet.
2. Rub. bands. (skinny)
3. Note: Loretta P. Sweeny going to kill Cindy on
           Sat.
           Loretta P. Sweeny watching P.
4. Just noticed: $3.42 in secret pocket.

CHAPTER 3

The bus doors opened and they jumped off. Abby grabbed Potsie by the arm. "Just stand here a minute and smell."

Potsie squinched her eyes shut and smiled. "Smells fishy, like the water. And popcorny. And . . ." She opened her eyes. "I can hear the kids yelling and the merry-go-round music."

It was always the same, Abby thought. She looked at the rough gray wood of the boardwalk that stretched out in front of her, and the long row of amusement stands.

She remembered coming here even when she was little, holding her mother's hand . . . going on the roller coaster with Dan . . . standing at the edge of the water.

The water. She shook her head. She wouldn't even think about getting in the water . . . being pushed off her feet by a wave . . . tasting the saltiness of it in her mouth.

"Let's go," she told Potsie.

She took the boardwalk steps two at a time, then threaded her way around a bunch of teenagers who were standing at the top.

She collided with Dan's friend Holly Monk.

"Sorry," she said, grinning at Holly's purple SUMMER IS FUNNER T-shirt, then started along the boardwalk.

"There it is" — she nudged Potsie — "the fortune-teller's booth."

She stared up at the booth with the stars and the moon painted on the top.

"We can't stand up here all day watching. . . ." Potsie began.

"Of course not. We've got to find a spot . . . somewhere under the —"

"How about we take a little swim first and then —"

"— under the boardwalk," Abby said firmly.

Potsie made a face. "It's all fenced in with wire."

"There must be holes in the fence," Abby said. "We'll go down on the sand, find a place to get in, and . . ." She tapped her foot on the boardwalk. "And sit right under this spot." She bent down and pulled off her sneakers. "Come on."

They hopped down the boardwalk steps and ran along the sand looking for an opening in the wire fence.

"Here," Abby said to Potsie, and tripped. Something large and bulky, wrapped in a blanket, lay in the sand.

Abby grabbed Potsie's arm. "Do you suppose . . ."

"A dead body?" Potsie asked at the same time.

The bundle moved a little. "Go away, kids, will you?" a voice said. A girl poked her head out of the top of the blanket. Abby could see part of her face — brown eyes, a nose slathered with white sunburn lotion, and a mouthful of silver braces. She had a pencil stuck behind one ear.

"Aren't you hot in there?" Abby asked.

The girl shook her head. "Just took a swim. Cold."

With Potsie right behind her, Abby stepped over the girl and ducked through the opening in the fence. She inched her way back into the dim coolness.

"There it is. Exactly right." She looked up at the spaces in the wooden boardwalk. "See the hot dog sign next to the fortune-teller's booth? And the souvenir stand. . . ." She broke off. "Good grief. Is that Dan? It *is* Dan."

Potsie looked up. "Working at the souvenir stand."

"I knew it. He gets into everything. Now he's going to be here gumming up the works, spoiling the whole mystery." She broke off and frowned. "Something just popped into my mind. Something I should be thinking of. Something with Dan? Something I was supposed to do?"

There was a slap of sneakers against the boardwalk. "Please," a voice called. "Is anybody there?"

Abby stood up and looked through the openings in the wooden planks of the boardwalk.

A small, plump woman was standing at the door of the fortune-teller's booth. She wore a green peaked hat over her gray hair, and her stockings were rolled down to the tops of her sneakers.

15

She banged at the door. "Please," she called again. "I need help."

"What's the matter?" Dan yelled from the souvenir booth.

"Where's Sister Amelia?" the woman asked, wringing her hands. "I've got to get her advice right away."

"I don't think she's there," Dan said.

The souvenir man leaned over the counter. The top of his bald head was all sunburned. "Sister Amelia is away," he said. "Princess Rita Rose is supposed to open up." He scratched the peels on his forehead. "I don't know where she's got to. She's not too reliable. Try tomorrow."

The woman wiped at her forehead. "My name is Mildred Pane," she said, "and I'm just desperate to see Sister Amelia."

Dan leaned forward. "What's wrong?"

"My friend," Mildred Pane said, her voice quavering, "Mrs. Upernicki. She's disappeared. Vanished."

"What happened?" Dan asked. "How —"

Just then the merry-go-round music started up.

Abby stood on tiptoes but she couldn't hear what Mildred Pane was saying. Finally the music stopped and the souvenir man said, "Better come back tomorrow."

Mildred Pane nodded uncertainly. "I guess you're right." She started to walk away. "That's what I'll have to do," she said over her shoulder.

CHAPTER 4

Abby looked at Potsie. "Mildred Pane," she said. "Maybe that's the 'P.' in the note."

Potsie clapped her hand over her mouth. "Now someone's been kidnapped," she said in a muffled voice.

"Come on," Abby said. "Let's see where she goes."

They scrambled through the opening and dashed across the hot sand.

In front of them, the girl in the blanket moved. "Hey, kid," she called to Abby. Her braces glinted in the sunlight.

Abby hesitated. "Me?"

"Come here for a second, will you?"

"I have to . . ." Abby began, looking at the stairs to the boardwalk.

"Please," the girl said. "Just a second."

Abby gritted her teeth. "Go ahead, Potsie. Hurry. I'll catch up."

She turned back to the girl.

"Do me a favor, kid?" the girl asked.

"I'm really in a hurry."

"You're going up to the boardwalk, aren't you?"

Abby nodded.

"Get me a Coke, will you? I'm dying of thirst." The girl closed her eyes.

"But . . ."

"Pay you when you get back. Get one for yourself. I'll pay for both of them."

"All right." Abby ran the last few steps across the sand and raced up on the boardwalk.

She spotted Potsie coming toward her.

"I lost her," Potsie said. "Right in front of the parking lot. I don't know whether she took a car or walked."

Abby stood there for a moment. Then she shrugged. "Never mind. She'll be back tomorrow. And we'll be right here waiting." She looked across at the souvenir stand. Dan was behind the counter talking to a girl, a teenager with huge, heart-shaped sunglasses. She was wearing a silly-looking yellow turban over her hair.

Abby and Potsie went a little closer.

"Bumper cars," the girl was saying. "That's my thing."

"Me, too," Dan said. "They're great."

Liar, Abby thought. Dan hated the bumper cars. He always said the noise gave him a headache.

"Health food, too," the girl said. "Absolutely. I'm careful about not getting sick. Eat a lot of alfalfa sprouts. Stuff like that."

"Asparagus," Dan said, and nodded.

Abby raised her eyebrows at Potsie. Dan hadn't eaten asparagus since he stopped eating baby food.

Abby looked at the stuff on the end of the counter. A real bunch of junk, she thought. She picked up a shell. It was marked "$1.00." She shook her head. You could walk right down to the edge of the water and pick one up for nothing. She looked toward the water. Maybe that's what they should do. Pick up some shells . . . paint them . . . sell . . .

Potsie nudged her. "Maybe we could get some shells. . . ." she began. "Start a business."

"Hey, kids," Dan said.

Abby looked up. "Hi."

"If you're not going to buy anything," he said, "better not touch."

"Huh," Abby said. "Think you're a big salesman now? King of the boardwalk?"

Dan turned to the girl with the heart-shaped glasses. "Have to watch out for these kids. They touch all the merchandise, then they don't buy a thing."

"I know," the girl said.

Abby stared at Dan. She put the shell down on the counter, and went over to lean against the railing with Potsie. "He's such a brat," she muttered.

Potsie looked toward the water. "Look, I'm melting from the heat. I've got to take a swim. Come on."

"Go ahead. I'll meet you under the boardwalk in a little while."

"Abby, you promised." Potsie put her hands on her hips. "Don't be such a coward."

"You should talk. The biggest scaredy-cat in the world. Besides, I've got things to do. I've got to get a soda for the mummy with braces. And I'm right in the middle of that book Garcia gave me for my birthday." She looked across the beach. "The water's a little rough-looking anyway."

Potsie stared at her accusingly. "It's as smooth as loose-leaf."

"I'll come in later. Really."

She watched as Potsie took off across the hot sand. "Get some shells," she yelled after her. Then she headed across the boardwalk to the hot dog stand.

She pulled her money out of her pocket and counted. "More than I thought," she told the frankfurter man.

"What'll it be?"

"Couple of Cokes and two franks," she said, watching the blue fortune-teller's booth out of the corner of her eye.

"Here, kid," the man said. "Pay attention." He handed her a cardboard box with the sodas and the hot dogs.

Abby reached for the mustard jar. "Know anyone named Cindy?"

The man thought for a moment. "Nah."

Abby covered the tops of the frankfurters with a thick yellow line of mustard. Then she licked the edge of her thumb and headed back down onto the sand.

The mummy with the braces was sitting up now, the gray blanket wrapped around her. Her long brown hair was wet and frizzy.

"Here's your Coke," Abby said.

"Great," the mummy said absently. "Just set it down there on my notebook."

Abby cleared her throat.

"Oh, the money," the girl said. She looked around.

"Gee. Sorry. Left my money home. Tell you what. I'll see you tomorrow. Pay you for both of them. All right?"

Abby glared at her, then she stepped over the edge of the blanket and went through the hole in the fence. She settled herself on her towel and pulled Garcia's book out of her knapsack.

CHAPTER 5

"Hey. Wake up."

Abby opened her eyes. "Milk," she said. "I was dreaming about milk." She sat up straight. "Good grief. I forgot the milk. When I went back for my knapsack, everyone was gone. I didn't even think. . . . My father probably didn't have any breakfast."

"What are you talking about?" Potsie asked.

Abby looked out at the beach. "Milk," she said again. "No wonder I had so much money before."

"I thought you were coming in the water," Potsie said. She dumped some shells on Abby's towel and looked down at her fingers. "I was floating around in there for so long I'm still all shriveled."

Abby picked up one of the shells. "Not so hot, Potsie. A little broken." She turned over another one. "I was reading Garcia's book before I fell asleep — the part about interrogating people."

"Interro — what?"

"Questioning. Like let's figure you're a prisoner. And I'm the detective. First I ask you —"

"Hey. What are you kids doing in there?"

Abby jumped.

In front of them, the girl with the heart-shaped sunglasses was setting up a blue umbrella. "You're not supposed to be in there."

Abby looked at Potsie. The girl was going to be a real pain in the neck. She cleared her throat and crawled over to the wire fence. "Did you ever hear of interrogatingitis?"

The girl shook her head.

"Nobody has. I mean practically nobody." Abby jerked her head toward Potsie. "My poor friend. At least this way she doesn't spread . . ."

The girl edged back in her beach chair. "It's catching?"

Abby lowered her head. "We'll just stay in here. Away from everybody. You know what I mean?"

The girl licked her top lip. "How long until she's better?" She hesitated. "Or . . ."

Abby waved her hand around. "She'll be all right in a couple of days. Three, I guess." She shrugged her shoulders.

The girl looked horrified. "She was swimming, wasn't she? Polluting up the water?" She stood up quickly and dragged her beach chair away from them across the sand.

"Hey, Abby, I'm starved," Potsie said from behind her. "I forgot all about lunch. It must be almost time to go home."

Abby turned. "Sorry. I forgot." She pushed the cardboard box over to Potsie. "I bought you a hot dog."

"Ugh," Potsie said. "That must have been ages ago. Look."

Abby leaned over. A fly was stuck in the mustard and the frankfurter was dried out and brownish-looking. "I think I have some Razzle-Dazzles or something in my knapsack."

She pulled the knapsack on her lap and began to fish through it. "Hey," she said, looking up. "Where's the rest of my money? I thought I put it in here when I came back from the frankfurter man. Don't tell me I dropped it in the sand."

"I don't even have enough to lend you," Potsie said. "I spent most of my allowance on earplugs. For swimming, you know? The water always gets in my ears." She shrugged. "Left them on the toilet tank. One of them fell right in. Whole allowance is gone for nothing."

Abby stuck her head in her knapsack. "Wait. There's a little left." She scooped up some coins. "Just enough . . ."

"Thank goodness," Potsie said. "I hate to walk."

"Just enough for a half gallon of milk," Abby said apologetically. "But you could take the bus alone if you want."

"It's all right," Potsie said. She looked down at her feet and wiggled her toes. "Poor old things."

"Thanks, Pots. I'll really make it up . . ." Abby broke off. "What's that?"

A few drops of water splattered on her back. She swiveled around.

A huge hairy brown dog was edging his way onto her towel. He was wet and full of sand.

"Look, Potsie."

Potsie didn't answer. She was crawling toward the hole in the fence as fast as she could.

"Potsie, come back. He's friendly."

Potsie glanced back over her shoulder.

The dog was licking Abby's arm.

Potsie waved her arms around. "Go home, dog."

The dog sniffed at Abby's knapsack and began to chew on the strap.

"Maybe he's hungry," Abby said. She pulled the knapsack away from him and opened it. "Razzle-Dazzles. Do you think a dog would . . ."

Potsie shook her head. "No."

"Never mind. There goes the frankfurter. Even the fly."

"Let's go home," Potsie said. "I'm hungry."

Abby rolled the shells into her towel and shoved them in her knapsack. "Good-bye, dog," she said, then crawled through the opening.

Up on the boardwalk, they sat on a bench to pull on their sneakers. As she tied her laces, Abby felt something cold against her leg.

The dog again.

He began to gnaw gently on the top of her sneaker.

She bent down and twisted his collar around. "There's a name. . . . It's worn off. . . . I can't quite . . ." She stared at it. "Super, I think. Yes, Super."

Potsie stood up. "Let's go."

They headed for the ramp, the dog right behind them. Abby turned. "Go back," she told him.

The dog stood there, panting a little, as they hurried down the ramp and crossed the street. "One day almost gone," Abby said, "and not one bit closer to finding that killer, Loretta P. Sweeny."

"And Cindy," Potsie added, "the girl she's going to kill."

Abby frowned. "And now there may be a kidnapping, too."

Halfway home, Potsie leaned against the telephone pole. "I hate this walk," she said, "especially when I'm starving to death."

"Not too much more," Abby said.

In back of them, someone screamed. Abby swiveled around. "Good grief. That dog again."

A little girl was looking at Super. She had an empty ice-cream cone in her hand.

Super was gulping down a big lump of orange ice.

"Super," Abby shouted. "Leave that alone."

Super licked his nose and loped toward them.

A woman came down the steps of the apartment house. "Why don't you watch your dog? Letting him loose like that. Kids like you don't deserve . . ."

Abby grabbed Potsie's arm and they started to run. They didn't stop until they were a block away from the apartment house.

"Nearly there now," Abby said breathlessly.

Potsie looked over her shoulder. "Hey. That dog is still following us."

Abby turned. "Go home," she yelled.

Just then a black cat started down the street.

Super barked once and began to chase it.

The cat streaked under a fence and jumped up on someone's windowsill.

Super, barking furiously, ran back and forth watching it.

"Let's go," Potsie said.

Quickly they ran the last block and pushed open the door to Abby's apartment house.

Kiki Krumback, the super's daughter, was kneeling in the middle of the lobby. She was dabbing gold paint all over a piece of cardboard.

"What's that all about?" Potsie asked.

Kiki stood up and pushed at her long red hair. "I'm designing a ballroom," she said.

Abby raised her eyebrows at Potsie as they stepped around the cardboard and headed for the stairs. "Can you imagine Mrs. Krumback if we started painting stuff in the middle of the lobby?"

Potsie shook her head. "That Kiki's got a short circuit in the brain."

Abby started up the stairs and stopped. "Oh, no," she moaned. "I forgot the milk again."

FROM THE MEMO BOOK OF
BRIDEY MONAGHAN (Irish)

DATE: Thurs. July 2.
TIME: Dawn.

Garcia's book says: Use the code *NEWOTY* when
you are working on a crime.

wheN: July 4

wherE: That's what I'd like to know

hoW: Knife? Gun (Terrible anyway.)

whO: Loretta P. Sweeny

whaT: Murder

whY: Maniac, probably.

P.S. New case: friend of lady nmd Mildred Pane.
(Mrs. Upernicki, or smthing like that.)

CHAPTER 6

Abby padded over to the window. Outside it was gray and cloudy.

It was a miserable day for the beach.

They'd have to go anyway and find out what was happening to Mildred Pane.

She went into the kitchen and pulled out the bread for sandwiches.

Her mother was bustling back and forth getting ready for work. "Did you make your bed?" she asked.

"Of course. Do you think I'd forget a simple thing like that?"

Her mother raised one eyebrow.

Abby gulped. "I know. You're thinking about the —"

"Milk," her mother finished for her.

"I'm sorry. I told you last night . . . I don't know how I —"

"Forgot such a simple thing?" her mother said, and grinned.

Abby grinned back at her. "Right."

"Did you straighten your room? Remember, Eggie's coming for dinner tonight." She reached over Abby's shoulder to shut the cabinet door.

"Great." Abby smiled. She had almost forgotten that Mrs. Eggler was coming. Eggie, their old baby-sitter, who believed that you could tell the future from dreams. Eggie, the worst cook, the worst housekeeper, but the nicest baby-sitter they ever had.

"Eggie wouldn't care if I didn't clean my room," Abby said.

Abby's mother nodded. "True. But I care. What are you going to do today anyway?"

"Going to the beach with Potsie."

"The beach?" Her mother looked out the window. "It's going to rain. In fact, I think . . ."

"Maybe it'll clear up," Abby said, crossing her fingers. She shoved the sandwiches into a brown paper bag, pecked her mother on the cheek, and looked at the clock. "Yikes. I've got to get out of here."

She tiptoed past her brother Dan's bedroom and out of the apartment. He'd probably sleep half the day. He'd never have to go to work in the rain.

Abby pushed open the heavy metal doors at the end of the hall and raced down the stairs to the lobby.

Potsie was standing next to the window peering out at the rain. She shook the curtain a little. "Do they ever clean these? Just look at the dust puffing out all over the place."

At that moment, Mrs. Krumback, the super, came in with her friend from the fifth floor. As usual, Mrs.

Krumback was wearing little pink rubber curlers in her hair. "It's just wonderful," Mrs. Krumback was saying. "We have a new dentist in the building." She stopped when she saw them. "What are you girls doing hanging around in here? Pulling on the drapes." She turned to her friend. "You can see summer is here. I dread it every year."

"We're leaving right now," Abby said. "We're going to the beach."

"The beach?" Mrs. Krumback's friend echoed. "It's pouring out."

Abby grabbed Potsie by the arm and started for the door.

"Impossible," Mrs. Krumback's friend said. "When I was a child, we did sensible things. On rainy days, we used to play jacks, or authors. We'd read a book. . . ."

"Or help our mothers . . ." Mrs. Krumback's voice trailed away as Abby opened the door and went out to the street.

For a moment, they hesitated on the top step. The rain was coming down in sheets. Already huddled under umbrellas, people were stepping around puddles on the sidewalk.

"Come on," Abby yelled. They tore down the steps, dashed to the corner, then stopped to catch their breath under the fruit man's awning.

"Whew." Potsie reached up to wipe a drop of rain off the end of her nose.

Abby gasped. "Where did you get that ring?"
"What?"

"That ring."

Potsie held her hand out and wiggled her fingers. "Gorgeous, isn't it?"

"Potsie, where?"

"Two dollars and . . ."

"Potsie."

"I bought it from Kiki Krumback last night when you were eating dinner. She said she didn't like it anymore, that someone said it didn't go with her red hair."

"It's the same kind of ring Loretta P. Sweeny was wearing," Abby said. "I saw it when she was going down the stairs."

"You don't think that Kiki . . ."

Abby shook her head. "Of course not. Kiki's not smart enough to plan a murder."

Potsie wiped another drop of rain off her forehead. "I saw someone else with a ring like this." She screwed up her face and shut her eyes. "Where was it?" Then she smiled. "I know. Down at the water's edge yesterday." She looked at Abby accusingly. "While you were sleeping, instead of swimming."

"Tell me," Abby said impatiently.

"I think it was that kid who was wrapped up like a mummy . . . the one with braces. She was down on her hands and knees looking around. I thought she had lost something, but she said she was looking for a shell."

"She should have been looking for her money. She owes me . . ." Abby frowned. "I should have noticed that ring myself. But she was all covered up in that blanket."

Potsie backed into a tray of tomatoes. "Oh, no. Look who's coming."

"Super," Abby said, looking at the dog who was lumbering toward them. "He must have been hanging around here since yesterday." She turned to Potsie. "I guess we can't take the bus now. We'll have to walk Super back to the beach so he can find his way home."

An hour later, huddled beneath the boardwalk, Abby squeezed some of the rain out of her sopping wet hair. She glanced up at the fortune-teller's booth for about the hundredth time. The door was closed tight.

"I can't stand it here another minute," Potsie said. "Mildred Pane isn't coming. There's no one here. No hot dog man, no souvenir man, nobody. Just us. And Super." She shoved at the dog. "Why does he have to lie all over me? He's gross. All wet and sandy . . ."

"There's one thing we could do," Abby cut in. "We could go right up there, knock on the door . . ."

"What?"

"Knock on the door," Abby said firmly. "Maybe someone's in there. I'll ask for a special reading. The cheap kind." She raised her eyebrows. "Maybe I can find something out."

Potsie shivered. "Let's make it fast. By the time we get home, we'll probably have pneumonia. I'll be ready for the hospital."

"Come on, Super," Abby said.

The dog just rolled his eyes and huddled farther back under the boardwalk.

"He doesn't like the rain," Abby said.

"Good," Potsie said. "Leave him here."

Abby patted Super on the head. "Good idea." She ducked through the opening and dashed across the wet sand.

Up on the boardwalk, she stopped to shake the sand off her sneakers. "Look at that," she told Potsie. "She's raised her prices." She reached into her pocket. "Good thing I brought a little extra for emergencies."

They hurried across the boardwalk and pulled at the little brass bell at the fortune-teller's booth.

Nobody answered.

Abby leaned forward, listening.

Suddenly the door opened a crack. It was so dark inside that all Abby could see was the edge of a long red dress and a dark veil.

"What do you want?" a voice whispered.

"I want my fortune told." Abby pushed a wet strand of hair out of her eyes. "Sister Amelia."

"Sister Amelia isn't here. Go away."

"Are you Princess Rita Rose? Can't you read . . ."

"Of course. Absolutely."

"Well then. Can we come in?"

A gloved hand reached out of the door and pointed to Abby. "Only you. Not her."

"Why?"

There was no answer.

Abby raised her shoulders a little and looked at Potsie. "Do you mind?"

"No, I love it out here in the rain. I'll go back and sit with Super. We can freeze to death together."

As soon as Potsie moved away, the door opened a little farther. "Come in."

36

Slowly Abby took a step inside. Even though she opened her eyes as wide as she could, everything seemed black.

She felt as if she were blind.

She couldn't see anything, not shadows, not even the figure who moved in front of her.

She could only hear the swish, swish of the long dress, and the sound of a footstep on the bare floor.

Suddenly there was another sound, then light. A candle glowed at one end of a table. And then at the other. They were so tiny, though, that Abby could just about see the table, and a dark curtain against the back wall.

"Sit," whispered the voice.

Slowly Abby sat down on a wooden bench in front of the table. In the center was a large bottle. It was filled with murky-looking water.

She leaned forward to get a better look.

There was something in the bottom of the bottle. It was long and tan. It looked horrible.

She wondered if it was alive. It lay there unmoving.

She swallowed. "What's that?"

For a moment, there was silence. Then the fortune-teller ran her hand over the rim of the bottle. "It is the force," she whispered. "It is the power. That's how Sister Amelia communes with the spirits."

"What about you?"

"And I also."

"But what is it?"

"Put your money on the table," the figure said in a faraway voice.

Abby reached into her wet jeans and put the money

on the table. "I guess I'm the first one here today,"
she said. "You haven't seen Mildred Pane yet, have
you?"

"Hummm," the voice said. The sound vibrated in
the tiny room. "Let me see your palm."

"Do you know someone named Sweeny?" Abby
asked, stretching her hand out to the fortune-teller.
"Loretta P. Sweeny?"

The fortune-teller made a sound. It almost seemed
to Abby that the gloved hand tightened against hers.

"I see trouble ahead for you," the fortune-teller
whispered. "Danger and difficulty. Problems and
panic. Fear and fate."

"What kind of problems?" Abby asked nervously.

"Problems on the beach."

"The beach?" Abby echoed.

"Watch out. Stay off the beach. Away from the
water. Away from the sand. Away from the boardwalk."

"But . . ." Abby began.

"Until after the Fourth of July. At least."

"But everything happens that day. The fireworks.
The play in the Little Theater . . ."

"Not for you." The fortune-teller let go of Abby's
hand and ran her fingers around the rim of the jar
again. "Tell your friend the same thing. It is even more
important for her. She'd better stay away from the
beach. Otherwise . . ." The figure stood up.

"Is that all?" Abby looked down at her money.

The gloved hand reached out and scooped up the
coins. "It is not good to know too much about the

future. Absolutely not." The figure turned and went behind the curtain.

Slowly Abby stood up.

At that moment, there was a sound from the back. Something slumped against the curtain.

As Abby stared, trying to see in the darkness, a thin line of red trickled out from under the curtain across the floor toward her.

CHAPTER 7

Abby moved backward until she felt the door. Then in an instant, she was outside, slipping across the wet boardwalk.

"Potsie," she shouted. "Hurry."

"Where are you going?" Potsie yelled from under the boardwalk.

"Bus stop. Got to get to Garcia. The station house." She tore down the ramp and headed for the street.

"I'm coming," Potsie yelled. "Don't leave me."

At the corner, she hesitated. There wasn't a bus in sight. She waited for Potsie and the dog to catch up. "We'll have to run for it," she said. "No time to wait for the bus."

Ten minutes later, her chest burning, she pushed open the station house doors.

The sergeant at the desk looked up at them. "Hi, girls," he said. "Too bad your friend Detective Garcia isn't here. He's in court. Testifying."

Abby took a deep breath. "Witkowski."

The sergeant raised his eyebrows. "You want to see Witkowski?"

Abby nodded. Everyone in the station house knew she didn't like Garcia's partner, Witkowski. But that was mainly because Witkowski didn't like kids. He had too many of his own, he said. All he wanted to do was to solve crimes and read his newspaper in peace and quiet.

The sergeant motioned toward the squad room at the back.

Abby rushed past him and banged open the door.

Witkowski was bent over his desk, his pale crinkly hair in a bush around his head. "Go away," he said. "Garcia's not here." He shook his head. "I knew that peace would be gone as soon as summer vacation began, but you don't even give me one day. . . ."

"I want to report a murder," Abby croaked.

Witkowski leaned back in his chair and slapped his forehead. "What next?" he asked the ceiling. Then he looked at Super. "Do you have to bring that flea-bitten thing in here?"

"Blood." Abby began to shake. "All over the floor."

Witkowski stood up and kicked a chair over to her. "Sit down. Relax your bones."

Abby collapsed into the chair. She could see her knees shaking.

"Relax, honey," Witkowski said. "Tell me what happened."

Abby jerked her head up. "Honey?"

Witkowski frowned. "Slip of the tongue," he said. "I was at the beach . . ."

"It's been pouring all day." Witkowski glanced toward the steamy window.

"We had something to check out."

"Go on."

"I went into the fortune-teller's booth," Abby said, wondering if Witkowski was interrogating them the way the book said. "I wanted my fortune told."

"I'll bet," Witkowski said.

In back of them, the door burst open. "Here I am," Garcia said. "Case closed. I lost." He smiled. "Hey. My favorite girls. . . ." He looked at the dog. "And . . ."

"And Super," said Potsie. "If there's a reward out for him, it's ours. We've been taking care of —"

"Her," Garcia broke in. "And she's chewing on Witkowski's umbrella."

"He's a she?" Potsie asked, moving the umbrella to the other side of the desk.

Abby stood up. "Oh, Garcia," she said. "I just saw a murder. Someone took a knife or something and . . ."

Garcia held out his arms and Abby stumbled over to him. She pulled at his sleeve. "You've got to come."

"Where?" Garcia asked.

Witkowski held up his hand. "Sister Amelia's and Madam whatever her name is."

"Princess Rita Rose," Abby said.

"What happened?" Garcia asked.

"We were watching her all day, then I went inside. She said there was going to be trouble. Panic and fear or something like that. She said we'd better stay away from the beach. Especially Potsie."

"Me?" Potsie squeaked. "She doesn't even know me. I knew it. Somebody's going to kill me next."

Witkowski put his hands on his head. "That kid is too much. She never shuts up and her voice is so screechy I can't stand to listen. . . ."

"Wait a minute," Garcia said. "What did you really see?"

"I heard a noise." She tried to remember. "A moan?"

"A moan," Potsie repeated. She clutched at her stomach.

"I saw something fall against the curtain. Maybe Princess Rita Rose. Maybe someone else." Abby raised her voice so they could hear her over Potsie's moans. "I saw a puddle of blood. I ran out of there so fast . . ." Her voice trailed off. "I left my knapsack on the table."

Garcia sighed. "Was there any money in it?"

"No. But your book, the detective book you gave me, some shells in a towel, and an egg sandwich or two. . . ."

"No," Potsie said. "Super finished them off."

"All right, girls," Garcia said. "My car is outside. Let's get your bag back." He looked at Witkowski. "Coming?"

Witkowski nodded. "This report is about two weeks late anyway. What's another day or two?"

Abby and Potsie followed them out the door with Super padding behind. "What about Super?" Abby asked.

"Squeeze her right in the back," Garcia said.

"Thanks," Witkowski said. "I love dog hair on my clothes."

"I'm not coming with you," Potsie said. "It's getting late."

Abby pushed Super into the back of the patrol car and climbed in. "Come on, Pots. Don't be afraid."

But Potsie shook her head, waved, then turned and raced down the street toward Washington Avenue.

Garcia stepped on the gas and pulled out of the parking space.

They were back at the beach in about five minutes. Instead of parking in the street, Garcia turned the wheel and drove the car up the ramp and onto the boardwalk.

Abby sat up straight, wishing there were people around, Dan especially, to see her driving around in a patrol car.

Garcia stopped in front of the blue booth and opened the car door.

"Can I come?" Abby asked. She started to push the front seat forward.

"Stay there," Witkowski said. He pushed open the door on the passenger side and followed Garcia to the blue door.

A few minutes later, they were back. Garcia was dangling the strap of her knapsack in his hand. "No problem. The fortune-teller's fine. No one else is in there." He grinned. "Dead or alive."

"What do you think was in that bottle?" Witkowski asked.

Garcia shrugged. "Disgusting-looking, wasn't it?"

Abby leaned forward. "Someone's finger, maybe?"

Garcia looked at her through the rearview mirror. "I'm surprised you didn't come in with us and take a second look."

Abby shot a look of anger at Witkowski's back. "I wanted to."

"Anyway," Garcia said, "there was no murder. Not a speck of blood on the floor. She said you must have imagined it."

As the car pulled away, Abby looked out the back window. She really had seen something on that floor. Maybe she should tell Garcia about Loretta P. Sweeny and Cindy and the murder.

But just then Witkowski started to laugh. "Blood," he said. "Murder. What next?"

Abby closed her mouth in a thin line. No, she wouldn't say a word. But she'd show Witkowski. She and Potsie would just have to solve the mystery all by themselves.

CHAPTER 8

"Is that you, Abby?" her mother called from the dining room.

"It's me, all right," Abby answered. She bent down and yanked off her wet sneakers.

Just then the phone rang.

Dan's door opened and he raced for it.

Abby made a face. "Think you're king of the boardwalk." She grabbed the phone.

"Abby?"

Potsie. Good.

"Listen, Pots," she said. "I can't talk now. I have to help with the dinner. Eggie's coming and you're invited. I meant to tell you yesterday."

"What are you having?" Potsie asked.

"Tongue."

"Sorry," Potsie said. "My mother . . ."

"I'm only kidding. It's spaghetti and meatballs."

Potsie laughed. "I'll be right over."

"Good. We've got plans to make. And listen, keep an eye out for Super on the way."

"Are you crazy?"

"Listen, Pots, Garcia let me out of the car on the corner and I thought Super was right behind me. . . ."

"Be glad he . . . she wasn't."

"I saw her cross Washington Avenue," Abby said. "Right in the middle of a whole bunch of traffic. She was lucky she wasn't killed."

"Abby," her mother called.

"I've got to get off, Pots." Abby hung up the phone and padded into the dining room. "Looks nice," she told her mother. "Flowers and everything."

"Daisies," her mother said absently. Then she looked up. "Turn the water down a little on the stove and —"

The doorbell rang.

Her mother smiled. "— and answer the door. That's probably Eggie."

A moment later, Abby was pulling Eggie into the apartment. "Don't fall over my sneakers," she said, looking up at Eggie's gray hair. Eggie's eyeglasses were perched on top of her head. They looked as if they were going to fall over her nose any minute.

Abby gave her a quick hug.

"Here," Eggie said. "A little dessert." She put a white box into Abby's hand.

"Chocolate cake?"

"Prune danish," Eggie said.

Abby's mother came down the hall. She almost collided with Dan, who was just coming out of his room. "Hiya, Egg," Dan said. "I got a job. Making money."

The door opened. It was Potsie and Abby's father coming in at the same time.

For a moment, everyone stood in the hallway talking at once.

Then Abby's mother yelled, "Spaghetti's ready. So am I. Everyone into the dining room."

"Still into dreams?" Abby's father asked Eggie when they were sitting around the dining room table.

"Getting better and better," Eggie said. "Tell me what your dream is and I can tell you what it means. I don't even need Madam Zera's dream book anymore."

"I dreamed a dog was going to bite me," Potsie said, as she passed the platter of spaghetti to Eggie.

"Then stay away from him," Eggie said. "Don't take chances."

Abby looked across the table at Potsie and narrowed her eyes.

Eggie turned to Dan. "Tell me about your job."

"Selling stuff," he said. "Sea horses, shells . . ."

"That reminds me," Abby said. "Suppose I had some shells to sell."

"Painted ones," Potsie added. "Really elegant."

Abby nodded. "Do you think the souvenir man might let us keep them on the counter? To sell?"

Dan laughed. "We have only special ones. Sand dollars, conches, stuff like that. Not junky ones like yours. Besides, he sends me down to the edge of the water every morning. I pick up any good ones I find."

Abby frowned at him. "Never mind. We'll sell them ourselves. Be rich long before you are."

Dan poked her in the arm. "Pass the meatballs."

"How come you're eating meat?" Abby rolled her eyes. "He just loves bean curds or alfalfa or whatever that health food stuff is."

"Shut up," he said. He gave her a kick under the table.

"His girl friend at the beach," Abby said, "the bumper car rider and health food nut thinks he's into all that stuff."

Her father laughed. "Who's the girl, Dan?"

Dan leaned over his spaghetti and shoveled a huge forkful into his mouth. "Nobody."

"She won't even sit near me on the beach," Potsie said. "She's afraid of germs."

"I don't blame her," Dan said. He looked at Potsie and pulled a long string of spaghetti into his mouth. "She'd probably get leprosy."

"Who?" Abby's mother asked. "What's her name?"

"Cynthia," Dan said. "And she's not my girl friend. I just saw her once."

Cynthia. Abby caught her breath. Cindy. "Does she have a nickname?" she asked.

"Have you had any dreams lately?" Eggie asked Dan at the same time.

Dan smiled at Eggie. "I dreamed I killed two bratty kids. Girls. Strangled them and threw them out the window."

"Really?" Eggie said, looking serious. "That was a terrible dream. A nightmare."

"Want to know their names?" Dan asked.

"Dan," his mother said. "That's not nice."

Abby put down her fork.

"Dan was only fooling," her mother said, frowning. "He really wouldn't throw you . . ."

"Cynthia," she said to Potsie.

Potsie broke off a piece of bread. "What?"

"Nickname . . ." Abby said, half choking on a piece of meat in her excitement.

"She's gone crazy," Dan said. "I knew it would finally happen. We'll have to lock her in a closet."

"What's a nickname for Cynthia?" Abby managed, still coughing.

"Cindy," Potsie gasped.

Abby nodded. Cindy. Cindy who was going to be killed on the Fourth of July.

Abby's mother pounded her on the back. "Take a drink of water."

Abby reached for the water and took a sip. She waited a moment. When she could finally talk, she turned to Dan again. "I have an important question. Do you know Loretta P. Sweeny?"

FROM THE MEMO BOOK OF
CATALINA MARTORANA (Italian)

DATE: Thurs. July 2.
TIME: In bathroom. Everyone else doing dishes.

THINGS TO BE DONE:
1.   Find out about blood in f. teller's booth.
          HOW?????
2.   Is Cynthia the one who's going to be mrdrd???
          FIND OUT. Smhow.
3.   Start own shell business.
          Could call business:
                    A & P Shell Business
                         or
                    Abpo's Souvenirs
                         or . . .
          (Mother calling. Mad because I'm taking too
          long in here.)

P.S. Have to remember to ask Dan what he knows
about Mildred Pane.

CHAPTER 9

"I'm hot," Potsie said. "Sticky."

"That's because we had to do about a thousand dishes. Happens every time we have company." Abby shoved up her bedroom screen. "The rain's stopped. Let's sit out on the fire escape. We have lots of things to talk about."

Potsie slid out the window behind her.

Together they leaned against the brick building and watched the street through the openings in the bottom of the fire escape.

"That Dan," Abby said. "He's in outer space somewhere. He never heard of Loretta P. Sweeny, doesn't even know if they call Cynthia Cindy, and he was probably hanging around with her for an hour."

"Maybe he's lying," Potsie said.

Abby shook her head. "No. I've been watching him lately. Every time he lies he sticks his tongue out a little. Looks as if he's catching flies."

She pulled her memo book out of her pocket. "I

made a couple of notes while I was in the bathroom. . . ."

"While I was stuck doing the dishes, you were taking your time in there, writing. . . ."

"First. We've got to find out about the blood in the fortune-teller's booth. I saw it, Pots, with my own eyes. Blood."

"No." Potsie shook her head hard. "I'm not going near . . ."

"Second. We've got to get to the girl with the heart-shaped glasses. Cindy. Warn her."

"I'm not going near the beach anymore."

"Third. We've got to get our shell business going."

"Only if you can find shells in the middle of Washington Avenue. You think I want to get killed going to the beach?"

Abby sighed. "I guess we can start with the shells you found yesterday. I have some paint from a Christmas present. . . ." She stood up. "Be right back. I'm going to get the shells. They're still in my knapsack."

A moment later, she ducked through the window again, dragging her knapsack. She sank down next to Potsie and began to fish through the knapsack.

"Hey," she said. "They're not in here."

Potsie leaned over. "Take everything out."

"Garcia's book. Some crumpled-up aluminum foil from the sandwiches. A bunch of sand on the bottom," Abby said, feeling the grit under her fingernails. "What a mess this is."

"They're wrapped in the towel," Potsie said. "Remember?"

"No. Look. The towel is empty."

They looked at each other.

"The fortune-teller?" Potsie said. "You think she stole . . ."

Abby nodded. "She certainly did." She began to put everything back into the knapsack. "That settles it."

"What?"

Abby ran her tongue over her lips. "Now listen, Potsie, don't say a word until you hear the whole thing."

"That means I'm not going to like . . ."

"It doesn't mean that at all. It means that you don't listen to what I'm trying to say. You always say no before I get a chance to . . ."

"I won't say a word," Potsie said. She folded her lips into a thin straight line.

"All right. What we have to do is go right into the fortune —"

"No."

"— the fortune-teller's booth. When nobody's there. See what caused that blood."

"Not me."

"See if someone's been murdered."

"I'm never going . . ."

"At the same time, we can get our shells back. When I think Princess Rita Rose had the nerve to steal . . ."

"You're crazy, Abby."

"The problem is," Abby said, digging the sand out from under her nails, "we have to get in there when no one's around. And . . ."

"Most of the time no one's there."

"And the only time we can really be sure that no one's there is at night."

Potsie stood up. "I'm going home. Right now. Right this minute." She stepped over Abby and started to duck through the window.

Abby grabbed her ankle. "Listen. I have the perfect plan."

Potsie sat down again.

"You heard Dan say he was going to the beach tonight to play softball." Abby grinned. "I think we should go with him. Keep my dear brother company."

Potsie pulled a dead marigold out of a pot and began to shred it. "He'll never let you go with him."

Abby stood up. "Just watch." She climbed through the window. "Come on."

In the dining room, Abby's mother and father and Eggie were still sitting around the table having coffee. Dan was standing in the doorway telling them about his job.

"Did you say," Abby asked, poking her head around him, "that you were going to the beach?"

"Playing softball," he answered. "My team is in second place. All we have to do . . ."

"Can I come?"

"No."

"Please?"

"All I need is a couple of dogs hanging around me. . . ."

"That's not nice, Dan," their mother said.

"I just want to watch a little softball," Abby pleaded.

Dan shook his head.

"I never get to go anywhere. Never mind. I'll just take the bus myself."

"No you won't," her father said. "Not at night." He

looked at Dan. "Let them go. Just keep an eye on them."

"I'm not going," Potsie said. "It's just Abby."

Abby glared at her.

Her father laughed. "See, Dan. It's only one dog. . . ."

"Daddy . . ." Abby said.

"I'm just kidding. I don't think you're a dog. Just a little joke," her father said.

"It's no joke," Dan said. "She's practically got fangs." He sighed. "All right. You can come. But don't say a word. Don't talk to me. Don't embarrass me. Just sit in the bleachers. . . ."

"I've got the idea," Abby cut in. "Are you ready?"

"Right now."

They followed him out the door and down the stairs. Outside, Potsie waved good-bye.

"Are you sure, Potsie?" Abby asked.

"You know what Princess Rita Rose said," Potsie answered.

"What?" Dan asked.

"Here comes the bus," Abby said. "See you tomorrow."

She climbed up after Dan and swung into a seat two rows behind him. She closed her eyes. She wanted to think about what she was going to do, how she was going to get into the booth, what she was going to find.

She just hoped Loretta P. Sweeny was far away.

CHAPTER 10

It was almost dark by the time they got to the softball field.

Abby slid onto the bleachers and looked up at the big lights. There were about a million bugs zipping around them.

"Meet me right here," Dan said, "after the game."

"All right," she said, still watching the bugs.

Dan spotted his friend Kevin Delio and walked toward him. She watched to see if he would look back at her, but he didn't.

In front of her, a couple of teenage girls were talking. Abby leaned forward. "There goes Dan," one of them said.

"Cute," Holly Monk said.

"Ears are a little big," the first one said.

"He's still cute," Holly said.

Abby edged off the bleachers. Still watching Dan over her shoulder, she hurried across the back of the field. Then she headed across Ocean Avenue and up the boardwalk ramp. She could see the moon and a couple of stars over the water.

She made a wide circle around the fortune-teller's booth. It looked deserted. Just to be sure, she went down on the sand and ducked through the opening in the wire fence.

The sand was still damp from the rain. It stuck to her sneakers. She tiptoed to a spot where she could see the booth.

Maybe it would be locked.

It probably was.

Maybe it would be just as well. Suddenly she wondered what would happen if she were caught.

She'd say she was trying to get her shells back, that the fortune-teller had stolen them.

It sounded dumb.

Too bad. It was true.

No one was there. Not a soul. She hurried back up on the boardwalk and tried the door.

Locked. Of course.

In a way, she was glad.

It was scary up here at night. There was no one on the boardwalk. No one, that is, except for a man and a woman, way down at the other end. They were walking a small white dog.

They wouldn't even hear her if she screamed.

Go back to the softball field, she told herself.

Sure, be a coward.

There must be another way into the booth.

There was a little alley between the booth and the souvenir man's stand. It was deserted, too. She'd make herself walk down the alley and see. Maybe there'd be another door or a window.

There was a window. Small and dusty. But just big enough for her to crawl through.

She pushed at it. It was stuck with paint. She banged at the sill, then stopped, hearing the noise she was making.

Once more she pushed. Suddenly the window slid open. She pulled her leg up over the sill and pulled herself inside.

It was pitch-black. She stood there leaning against the back wall. If only she had a flashlight.

She held her arms out and took a step forward. She could feel the curtain in front of her.

She nodded to herself, remembering the curtain and the blood that had dribbled out across the floor.

Cautiously she bent down and felt the floor. Garcia was right. It was dry. But it would be dry anyway. It was hours since she had been here.

She waved her arms around until she felt an opening in the curtain, then inched her way forward.

She bumped into the table. With her fingertips, she could feel the large jar with the water. She shuddered, thinking about what must be in that bottle.

She'd have to find out.

She'd never be able to reach in. Suppose it was alive. Suppose it was something horrible. A finger. Or . . . Better not think about it.

Carefully she picked up the bottle and stepped back, past the curtain, over to the window.

The moon was up higher now, lighting the back of the boardwalk. She could see the ramp and the softball

field beyond it, but it wasn't bright enough to get a good look into the jar. She held the jar up and squinted. A little of the water sloshed over the side.

She wiped her hand on her jeans. Disgusting.

She tilted the jar a little. The thing inside moved, clinked against the glass.

It was hard. Funny, she figured it would be soft and slimy.

She poured a little more of the water out. The thing slid toward the top of the jar. The end was tan with darker spots.

A shell.

Just a miserable old shell. And broken, too. It was in pieces.

Suddenly she heard footsteps. In front of the booth? Coming down the alley?

She couldn't tell.

Quickly she pushed through the curtain and reached for the table with her foot. She slid the jar onto the table and edged back to the curtain.

A dog barked.

She took a deep breath. It was probably the man and the woman and the little white dog.

She waited until she couldn't hear the footsteps anymore, then she put her leg over the sill and climbed outside.

She wondered what time it was. She couldn't tell if she had been inside a few minutes or an hour.

It seemed forever.

Head down, she started for the alley. She really hadn't learned anything much. If only she had brought a flashlight. If only . . .

Suddenly there was a sound from the other end of the alley. She jumped back and flattened herself against the wall of the fortune-teller's booth.

"Just a little longer," a voice said, "and Cindy will be finished."

"You know," said the other voice. "I never felt sorry for her sister before, but now I'm glad you're going to kill . . ."

"Half sister. Parents are divorced. Remember? But right now, I'm worried about that junonia."

Abby drew in her breath. She stood there for a moment. Then she raced down the alley. But it was too late. The boardwalk was empty.

DATE: Thurs. night.
TIME: Very late.

KILLER HAS HELPER. A FIEND.
Cindy has a half sister. Must ask Dan about.

What's a junonia . . . jerolia . . . unjonia? KILLER
NEEDS ONE.

CHAPTER 11

Abby sat on her fire escape watching the early morning traffic. She could hear Dan's radio blaring. The weatherman said it was going to be a scorcher.

She didn't need the weatherman to tell her that. It was going to be a horrible day. Her hair was plastered to her head and her shirt was glued to her back.

It was too hot to spend the day thinking about Loretta P. Sweeny.

It was too hot to think about anything.

Except that the Fourth of July was tomorrow.

They had just one day left to save Cindy's life.

She sat there a while longer, watching the people below on their way to work; then she swung herself back through the open window. She threw a towel into her knapsack, then went down the hall to the kitchen.

Her mother was sitting at the table stirring a cup of coffee.

She looked up at Abby and grinned. "Tomorrow is Fourth of July," she said. "Dad and I are closing the car lot for the day. I'm going to spend the whole time on the beach asleep."

"Sounds good," Abby said.

"Except for the fireworks." Her mother took a sip of coffee and made a face. "Too hot for coffee. And I might go up on the boardwalk to see the play in the Little Theater."

"What is it this year?"

Her mother shrugged and stood up. "I'm not sure. Daddy said it was a mystery, but someone told me it was a fairy tale." She opened the refrigerator. "We have some cheese. Maybe I'll make macaroni and cheese for supper."

"I think I'm going to be sick."

"How about eggs?"

"Worse."

"Hot dogs then."

"Terrific."

"You'll have to get them at the store."

Abby grinned. "Macaroni and cheese. Good, I love it."

Her mother laughed. "See you later. I'm late. Daddy left about twenty minutes ago. He had to meet a customer." She hurried down the hall.

Abby took a long swallow of orange juice out of the container and reached for a box of Doo Dads.

Her mother's voice floated back. "And don't leave your cereal bowl in the sink. Those krispies stick like glue."

"Dan's the one . . ." she began, but her mother was gone.

Ten minutes later, Abby crossed the street and marched into Potsie's room. "Come on, get up. We have to get down to the beach. Warn Cindy that she's going to be murdered tomorrow."

Potsie pulled her pink quilt up to her chin.

"It must be ninety degrees in here," Abby said.

"Maybe a hundred," Potsie agreed.

"What's the matter with you?"

"Princess Rita Rose said . . ."

"Don't you want to hear about last night?"

Potsie sat up. "Did you . . ."

Abby nodded. "First I heard someone talking. I knew right away from the voice that she was a killer."

"Loretta?"

"Of course, Loretta. And her partner, too. Cold. Dangerous. Talking about something called a junonia, whatever that is." She took a breath. "Potsie, they'll stop at nothing. Nothing. I just about escaped with my life."

"Maybe we should go to . . ." Potsie began.

"Don't say police," Abby said. "We're going to solve this yet, Potsie. You'll see." She pushed her hair back off her forehead. "Come on, Pots. We have to go to the beach. It's too hot in here."

Potsie sank down in the bed a little. "Panic and fear. Remember." She looked out the window at the sunlight. "A knife probably. Maybe a gun."

Abby leaned against the dresser. "Don't be silly."

High heels clicked down the hall. Potsie's mother

stuck her head in the doorway. "You have a dentist's appointment in a half hour, Potsie," she said. "With that new dentist in Abby's building. I left the money on the kitchen table."

Potsie stared at her mother. "I think I'd better cancel. I don't feel so —"

"I'll break your arm," her mother said cheerfully. "Want your teeth to fall out by the time you're twelve?" She tapped on the doorway. "Love you," she said. "Love you both. I'll be home from work by five."

She clicked down the hall again.

A moment later, Abby heard the front door close behind her.

Potsie looked at Abby. "I'll go as far as the dentist," she said. "Just across the street to your apartment house." She shook her head. "Not to the beach. Not even as far as the corner."

Abby sighed. "We'll talk about it after the dentist. Get dressed."

Ten minutes later, a blast of cold air hit them as they opened the door to Dr. Moore's office.

"Whew." Abby pulled at her shirt. "Feel that air conditioning."

"Smell that dentist smell," Potsie said. "Ugh."

Abby looked around. Everything looked new: the blue rug, the leather couch, the striped wallpaper.

Dr. Moore's nurse sat at a shiny desk in the corner. She looked like an old teenager. She had on tons of makeup and she was wearing a ring. A Loretta P. Sweeny type ring.

Abby went up to the desk. "Nice ring," she said.

The nurse looked down at her hand. "Got it at the

beach. There was a whole tray of them at the souvenir stand the other day."

"Lose anything lately?" Potsie asked.

"Like what?"

"A wallet," Abby said.

The nurse shook her head.

For a moment, Abby watched the purple ring glinting in the light. Then she reached for a magazine in the rack next to the desk. She pretended to be interested in the picture on the front cover. It was a drawing of someone's gums with a couple of long teeth hanging down.

"HAVE YOU FLOSSED TODAY?" was written in red letters underneath.

Abby ran her tongue over her teeth. She couldn't remember when she had flossed last. She wondered if she had even brushed her teeth this morning. She'd hate to look like that picture in a couple of months or so.

The dentist stuck his head out of the inside office. He had a dark fuzzy beard. "Penelope Olivia," he said.

Potsie giggled. "Potsie." Slowly she started toward him.

The dentist grinned. "You'd better come in with her," he told Abby. "Keep her company. She looks as if she might run away any minute."

Abby followed Potsie inside and sat down on the window ledge.

"You'll hardly feel this, really," he said. "Open your mouth."

Potsie squinched her eyes shut and opened her mouth a little.

"That's fine," he said. "If I were an ant I could get my fingers in your mouth easily."

Potsie rolled her eyes at Abby and opened her mouth a little wider.

The dentist reached for a long skinny-looking pick and began to poke around Potsie's back tooth.

Abby shut her eyes for a moment. She could feel her hands getting wet.

The dentist started the drill. It had a high, whiny buzz. Abby shuddered. She was going to remember to brush her teeth from now on. Five or six times a day.

"Just empty," the dentist told Potsie after a minute or two.

Potsie leaned over the little sink. "Almost finished?" she asked, wiping her mouth.

"Almost."

Abby looked out the window. The dentist was humming as he stuck a whole bunch of cotton in Potsie's mouth. Abby wished he'd hurry up. The whole morning was being wasted. And they had such a little bit of time left.

"Glumpf," Potsie said.

Abby turned back to look at her. Her cheeks were puffed out like a chipmunk's.

"Another minute," the dentist said.

Potsie mumbled something again and pointed to the dentist's tray.

"I finished drilling," the dentist said. "It can't hurt."

"Mnf," Potsie mumbled and pointed to the tray again.

"My equipment?" the dentist asked. "Brand-new. Three weeks old. I just started . . ."

Abby stood up and looked at the tray. She opened her eyes wide. "What are those?"

He looked down. "Which?"

"Rubber bands," Abby said.

Potsie nodded.

The dentist picked up one of the little rubber bands. It lay there in his palm. Small. Fine. "For braces," he said. "We use this to attach the top braces to the bottom ones. Here." He held it out to Abby. "Take one if you like."

For a moment Abby and Potsie looked at each other. Then the dentist took the cotton out of Potsie's mouth and Potsie leaned over the sink again.

A few minutes later, Potsie shot out of the chair, and they hurried out of the office. When they reached the hall, Abby held up the rubber band. "Just like the ones in Loretta P. Sweeny's wallet."

"Exactly," Potsie said.

"What a clue," Abby said, dancing around. "Now we know that the killer has braces."

"But lots of kids wear braces."

"Yes, but the murderer isn't a kid," Abby said slowly. "Wait. Let me think."

She looked at the rubber band. "Silver braces. I saw them. But where?" She drew in her breath. "The mummy in the gray blanket. At the beach. She's no kid, Potsie, and she was wearing braces."

"The murderer?"

Abby nodded. "Loretta P. Sweeny herself."

"Watching us," Potsie said.

"No. Watching Cindy. Now we've really got to get to the beach. Tell Cindy. Before it's too late."

Potsie clamped her lips together and shook her head.

"You want to be the cause of a murder?"

For a moment, Potsie stood there, her lips trembling a little. Then she sighed. "All right. I'll go with you."

Abby punched the elevator button, then shook her head. "No time." She headed for the stairs. "We'll get our knapsacks and get down to the beach as fast as we can."

FROM THE MEMO BOOK OF
SOPHIA MAIJEWSKI (Polish)

DATE: Fri.
TIME: On way to bch.

KILLER:
1. Wears braces.
2. Has purple ring.
3. Name: Loretta P. Sweeny.

MUMMY ON BEACH:
1. Wears braces.
2. Has purple ring. (Potsie saw on bch.)
3. Name: Has to be Loretta P. Sweeny. (I think.)

CHAPTER 12

From the boardwalk, Abby looked over the beach. "Don't worry," she said. "Loretta P. Sweeny's not around."

"Thank goodness," Potsie breathed.

"Neither is Cindy."

"Maybe the bumper place?"

"Let's try," Abby said.

They hurried back to the street and stopped at the low wooden fence. Only one bumper car was going around the track.

The girl in heart-shaped sunglasses was driving. When she saw them watching, she zoomed down the track toward them, her arm loose across the top of the steering wheel.

Abby jumped back.

At the last minute, the driver flicked her wrist a little and the car turned away from them.

"That's Cindy, all right," Abby said, frowning. "Come on."

They walked over to the ticket booth. Dan's friend Kevin Delio was inside. He was reading a motorcycle magazine.

"Can we go around to the bumper cars?" Abby asked. "I want to talk to that girl."

He looked at them. "One buck."

"We're not going to ride," Abby explained. "I just want to talk . . ."

He turned the page of the magazine and began to read again. "A buck," he said.

Abby measured the distance between the booth and the little gate to the bumper cars. "Come on, Potsie," she said, and dashed down the aisle.

"Come back here," Kevin yelled. "Want me to lose my job?"

"Cynthia," Abby yelled, waving her arms around.

But Cynthia was careening down the opposite side of the track. The noise was deafening.

"Cynthia," Potsie screamed.

"Out," the boy yelled.

At that moment, Cynthia turned and came down the track toward them.

"Cynthia," Abby screamed again.

Cynthia slid to a stop in front of them. "What are you two doing here?"

"We've got to talk to you," Abby said.

"So talk," Cynthia said.

"You're supposed to pay," the boy said.

"Pair of weirdos," Cynthia said. "I'll get rid of them in a second."

The boy shrugged and went back to the booth. "No wonder we're losing money," he muttered.

Potsie leaned forward. "We're just trying to save your puny little life."

Cynthia backed up the car a little. "Stay away from me," she said. "I don't need to catch your germs."

"What we're trying to say," Abby began, "is that someone —"

"Is trying to kill you," Potsie broke in. "Stab you or strangle . . ."

Behind the sunglasses, Cynthia's eyes widened. "Now I know you're crazy. Your disease has scrambled your brains."

"Potsie's right," Abby said. "You've got only a short time left."

Cynthia stood up in the bumper car. "I'm going to count to three. Then I'm going to get Kevin to come after you. I don't know how you dare come to the beach anyway. One!"

"You've got to listen," Abby said.

"Two!"

"I read it. It was in a —"

"Three!" Cynthia started to yell. "Kevin . . ."

"Here we go," yelled Abby, and tore down the aisle with Potsie right in back of her.

They didn't stop to catch their breath until they reached the souvenir stand.

"Keep your eyes open," Abby said, "for Loretta P."

Potsie nodded. "I'll die if I see her. She won't even have to kill me."

In front of the souvenir stand, Dan was yelling, "Live sea horses. Raised special." He looked up and saw them. "How are the great detectives today?" he called. "Solve anything lately?"

Two women strolling along the boardwalk turned to stare at them.

Abby narrowed her eyes at Dan. "Don't pay any attention to that pinhead," she told Potsie.

"Don't worry," Potsie said.

"What are we going to do about Cindy?" Abby asked. "We just can't let her be killed."

"I know what we're going to do." Potsie put her hands on her hips. "Go swimming."

Abby looked out at the water. Today it was blue. Sparkling. About a million kids were playing around at the water's edge. "I don't . . ." she began.

"You promised," Potsie said. "If you want to be my friend . . ." She broke off. "I came down to the beach, right? Even though I was afraid."

Abby felt a drop of perspiration roll down her back.

"I mean it," Potsie said.

"For a few minutes." Abby started down the ramp behind Potsie and plodded along on the hot sand. She tried not to think about that other time — the time that she had been in the water with Dan and her father. They were teaching her how to swim. Holding her. Smiling. Then suddenly a wave roared in at them. She felt their hands slip away from her. She went under, swallowing great mouthfuls of water, feeling her lungs about to burst. . . .

She stopped at the water's edge.

Potsie was in already, looking like a seal with her wet hair slicked back and the water dripping off her face. She smiled encouragingly. "Just dash right in. Get yourself wet."

As a tiny wave curled toward her, Abby took a few

steps forward. She put one foot into the edge of the foaming water as it raced up on the sand.

It was cold. Freezing. Wonderful. She waded in until she felt it lapping at her knees.

Potsie rolled over on her stomach and began to swim toward her. "Very good," she said. "Now all you have to do is lie on your stomach and . . ."

Gingerly Abby knelt down.

"Stretch out," Potsie said, sounding like a general.

Abby leaned over a little. She could feel the water against her stomach. She shivered.

"Good," Potsie yelled. "Great."

Abby dug her toes into the sand.

"Move your arms," Potsie said.

Abby raised one arm over her head. Her fingers sliced into the water and hit the sand on the bottom. Nothing to it, she told herself.

"Kick your feet," Potsie yelled. "Hard."

Slowly Abby raised one leg and gave a little kick.

"Are you kicking with both feet?" Potsie asked.

Abby opened her mouth. A wave filled it with water. She reached down and grabbed at the sand with both hands.

"That's enough," she sputtered. She stood up and scrambled toward safety.

Potsie followed her out of the water. "Enough? You were in there about a quarter of a minute."

Abby sank down on the wet sand and tried to catch her breath. After a moment, she looked around. "We've got to find some shells," she said. She stood up and walked along the water's edge, gathering them up.

"Here's a nice one," Potsie said. She handed it to

Abby. Long and tan with dark brown spots, it had a soft shine.

"Neat," Abby said, hands full. "Hey. It looks like the one I saw in the fortune-teller's bottle."

She sat down. "I guess we have enough for a start." She began to push some of the sand into a little hill. Then she made a moat around it.

Potsie leaned over to help her.

Ten minutes later, they were finished. There was a castle with a moat and a drawbridge and little sand soldiers. Abby stuck the tan and brown shell up on top of the castle.

"Pretty," Potsie said.

Suddenly Abby looked up. "What dummies we are. I just realized, we missed an important part of the rubber band clue."

"If we could just get the water to come into the moat," Potsie began.

"Potsie, stop. Listen to me. We know that the mummy is Loretta P. Sweeny, right?"

Potsie looked up. "Right."

"And we know that she wears braces."

"Right."

"And I found her wallet on the stairs."

Potsie nodded impatiently. "Yes. I know all that."

"I'll bet," Abby said slowly, "that Loretta P. Sweeny is one of Dr. Moore's patients. She probably had an appointment the other day. Then she took the stairs down . . ."

"And dropped her wallet on the way out," Potsie finished. "You're right. Absolutely."

Abby wrinkled her forehead. "Someone else says

absolutely all the time." She shrugged. "Anyway, Potsie, now we really have a place to begin." She stood up.

"Where?"

"We've got to go home. Plan." Abby picked up their pile of shells and started across the sand. "Somehow we've got to get into the dentist's office. We'll be able to get Loretta's address . . . her telephone number . . ."

Potsie grinned. "Her X rays."

Abby grinned back. "At least we'll get some good solid evidence."

Halfway to the boardwalk, Abby stopped.

"What now?" Potsie asked.

"I forgot that shell. The one that looked like the fortune-teller's." She raced back across the sand.

There was a skinny girl leaning over the castle, reaching for the shell.

Abby dodged around her, grabbed it, and raced back across the sand. "Sorry," she yelled, not even looking back. "It's mine."

/

DATE: Fri.
TIME: On bus coming hme from bch.

Garcia's book says: USE THIS PROFILE TO DESCRIBE
SUSPECT.

Name:	Loretta P. Sweeny
Height:	Tall
Weight:	Kind of skinny
Distinguishing marks:	Braces (Good thing or we'd never have found her.)
Hair:	Brown
Eyes:	Brown
Other information:	Wants junonia thing.

Killer's Helper

Name:	Don't know.
Height:	Dn't kn.
Dist. marks:	Dn kn
Hair:	D k
Eyes:	dk
Other info:	Horrible type

CHAPTER 13

Two hours later, Abby stepped around the shells on her bedroom floor and handed a Coke to Potsie. "They look great," she said. "All painted up like that. Red. Blue . . ."

"I'm glad we didn't paint the tan one, though. It looks nice just the way it is."

Abby took a slurp of her Coke. "Now let's go over this again. Make believe you're the dentist's nurse," she said. "I say 'I just heard my old friend Loretta P. Sweeny is a patient of yours.' "

Potsie nodded. " 'That's right, my dear.' "

Abby giggled. " 'How about giving me her address?' "

In the hall, the phone rang.

Abby dashed to get it. "Jones residence," she said in her best maid's voice.

"Is Dan there?"

"Uh-uh."

"Give him a message. Tell him I still need the junonia."

Abby drew in her breath. "Who is this? What's a junonia?"

For a moment, there was silence. "Who is this?" the voice asked.

"Abigail Jones," Abby said. "I live here."

There was a click. Abby looked at the phone. Then she put it gently in the cradle.

She licked her lips. Was that Loretta P. Sweeny? Imagine. A murderer calling her own house. Knowing her own brother. That was the trouble with Dan. He had a skillion friends. He probably knew everyone on the beach by now. Too bad he didn't pay attention to which ones were criminals.

"Who was that?" Potsie called.

"Nobody." Abby went back into the kitchen. If Potsie ever found out that Loretta P. Sweeny knew where they lived, she wouldn't get out of bed for the rest of the summer.

"What do you mean nobody?"

"Someone for Dan."

Potsie giggled. "That's nobody?"

Abby smiled back a little weakly. "Just about," she said. She swallowed. Her throat felt dry. "We were talking about the dentist," she said as she reached for her Coke, "and how we were going to get Loretta's address."

She wondered if Dan knew Loretta's address. She wondered why he had said he didn't know Loretta. Just last night. And she had believed him.

90

"Best thing to do," she told Potsie, "is to get right up to the fifth floor. . . ."

"I told you Dr. Moore's hours are over at three. It's after five now."

"And I said maybe the door is open or something. We could just take a look."

Potsie thought for a moment; then she slid off the table. "All right. I'll go with you."

They started for the front door.

From the outside, someone pushed the door open.

Abby jumped.

Dan.

"What are you doing home?" she asked. "Trying to scare us?"

"Scare the big detectives?" Dan grinned. "Boy, if you really had a case . . ."

"We certainly do have a . . ." Abby began and broke off. "What's a junonia?"

"Look in the dictionary." He brushed past them.

"Come on, Dan," she said, following him down the hall. "Tell . . . Hey. That reminds me. I've been meaning to ask you for the last two days. . . . What do you know about Mildred Pane?"

"The fat lady? Gray hair?"

"Right."

"Green hat? Stockings rolled down . . ."

Abby nodded impatiently.

"Never heard of her." Dan started to laugh. He clapped her on the back.

"Don't be so dumb," Abby said. "This is important."

Dan shrugged. "I think she's looking for someone."

"And . . ." Abby prompted.

"And nothing. She was talking to Princess Rita Rose about it before." He opened his bedroom door. "Wouldn't you like to know what's going on?" He grinned at them and closed the door behind him.

"Brat face," Abby said.

Dan opened the door a crack. "Her friend's probably dead," he said. "Thrown in the water. Drowned or something like that."

"And we're swimming right in there?" Potsie squeaked. "Right in with a dead . . . floating around. . . ."

"I told you we shouldn't be swimming," Abby said. "I told you that right from the beginning. You could reach right down and come up with an arm or a leg or maybe even a head."

Dan closed the door again. They could hear him laughing as he threw himself on the bed.

"He was just joking," Abby said. "At least I think . . ." She broke off and opened the front door, wondering if she should tell him about the phone call. Then she shrugged. He shouldn't be talking to murderers anyway.

"Come on, Pots," she said. "My mother and father will be home any minute. Let's get a move on."

They let themselves out of the apartment and tiptoed up the stairs to the fifth floor.

The door to Dr. Moore's office was open.

Pressed against the wall, they peered in at the dentist's nurse. She was talking on the phone, playing with the telephone cord. Abby could see her purple ring flashing in the light.

"Sorry," the nurse said. "I'm going to be a little late.

We had emergencies all over the place. Dr. Moore just left. I have to straighten up, put everything away. . . ."

Abby looked at Potsie. "Should we ask . . ."

Just then the nurse put the phone down, stood up, and headed for Dr. Moore's room.

"Maybe you could go in there," Abby said. "Talk to her. Change your next appointment or something like that."

"I thought we were just going to ask for Loretta's address," Potsie said.

Abby frowned. "Suppose she doesn't tell us. No, it's better if we just . . ."

Potsie nodded a little uncertainly.

"Keep her in the other room. I'll take a look at the book."

Potsie wiped her hands on her shorts. Then she marched across the office and opened the door to Dr. Moore's room.

The nurse screamed.

"I didn't mean to scare you," Potsie said in a loud voice. She went into the room and half closed the door behind her.

"That's all right," the nurse said, frowning a little. "What do you want?"

Abby rushed over to the desk. The big appointment calendar was right on top of the desk. She leaned over to take a look.

She could hear Potsie mumbling something to the nurse about her next appointment, and wanting to take diving lessons, and maybe she should change her appointment, but then again she didn't want to bother . . .

No Loretta P. Sweeny. Not this week, not last week, and not next week.

How could that be? Abby had seen her on the stairs last Monday.

Kiki Krumback, the super's daughter, had had an appointment yesterday.

Her own father had one for the seventh of July.

But there was no Loretta P. Sweeny. No Sweenys at all.

"I'll have to look in the appointment book," the nurse said from inside.

"No, that's all right," Potsie said. "Never mind."

"Don't mind at all," the nurse said. "Where's your friend today?"

"She's around," Potsie answered.

Abby heard the nurse's footsteps coming toward her. There was no time to run outside.

She dove under the desk.

The nurse came closer, stopped in front of the desk. She screamed again.

But this time, the scream was louder and it seemed as if it would never stop.

CHAPTER 14

Abby poked her head up from under the desk. "I didn't mean to scare . . ." she began.

But the nurse wasn't looking at her. She was staring, horrified, at the huge brown dog in the doorway.

Super. How had she gotten there? She had a dirty green sock hanging out of her mouth.

The nurse backed into the inside office and slammed the door behind her.

Abby could hear her dialing the phone. "Mrs. Krumback," the nurse screamed. "A dog. An attack dog, I think. Ready to lunge . . ."

Abby scrambled out from behind the desk. "Come on, Potsie," she said, "we've got to get Super outside before Mrs. Krumback gets up here."

She gave the dog a little push. "Let's go, Super."

They headed for the elevator, but already the little arrow was moving up from 1.

Mrs. Krumback was on her way.

Abby tore down the hall with Potsie and Super right behind her. She banged open the door to the stairway.

Halfway down, they could hear the sound of footsteps coming up.

Abby looked over the railing. It was Kiki Krumback. When she saw Abby's head, she yelled up, "There's a rabid dog in the building. Run for your life."

"I will," Abby said.

As Kiki stamped up toward them, Abby looked around wildly.

They were almost to the second-floor landing. Abby dashed down the last two steps and opened the door to her floor. They'd have to duck into her apartment. She just hoped her mother and father weren't home yet.

Quickly she unlocked the door. And pushed it open.

Nobody was home. Nobody except Dan. And he was in his bedroom, listening to the radio. The whole apartment was vibrating from the noise.

Abby led the way down the hall and closed her bedroom door behind Potsie and Super.

"Watch out," she said.

"Too late," Potsie said.

They watched as Super crunched over a row of bright blue shells and climbed up on Abby's bed.

"Good grief," Potsie said. "She's just ruined most of our business. Only three reds and a tan left."

"Paint's still wet," Abby said, looking at a blue paw mark on her spread. "Good thing the spread is plaid."

With a sigh, Super curled herself into a big round lump and closed her eyes.

"Now what?" Potsie asked.

Abby looked at the dog. "If my mother could see her asleep on my bed . . ." She shook her head thinking of Dan's allergies. "We've got to get her out of here." She grinned to herself. Too bad they just couldn't get rid of Dan instead.

"Anybody home?" her mother yelled from the end of the hall.

Abby drew in her breath. Then she opened the door a little and stuck her nose out. "I'm here. And Potsie, too."

"So is Dan," her mother said. "I can tell by the radio."

Abby closed the door again. "Potsie, we'll have to do something about this dog."

Potsie sat on the edge of the bed and pulled the corner of Abby's bedspread out of Super's mouth. Gingerly she reached out and patted the dog with the tips of her fingers. "Do you think we should take her back to the beach?"

"The beach?" Abby asked absently. She took the dictionary off her desk.

"The beach," Potsie repeated. "Are you paying attention? I think Super got all mixed up when she followed us here the other day. If we bring her back, maybe she'll be able to start all over again, find her way home."

"But what will we do with her tonight?" Abby flipped through the dictionary pages.

Potsie looked at the door and bit her lip. "Do you think you could keep your door closed? Maybe your mother wouldn't notice."

"I'd never get away with it," Abby said. She slammed the dictionary shut and glanced at the window. "Maybe we could put her out on the fire escape. We could spread out a blanket or something for her to lie on."

"With half the apartment house looking for a dog with rabies?"

"You're right," Abby said. "We'll have to keep her in here. Maybe by some miracle, my mother won't notice."

"Abby," her mother called.

"Coming."

Quickly Abby opened the door a little and slipped through.

Her mother was in the kitchen. "Hot," she said. "Too hot to cook." She brushed her hair off the back of her neck. "How about running down to Wing Lee's. Get some spare ribs and fried rice."

"What about Dan? Doesn't he ever have to go to the store anymore?"

"Be fair," her mother said. "He worked all day. He's tired and sunburned."

Abby sighed. "It's always me." She took the money off the counter and went back to the bedroom. She stuck her head in the door. "I have to go down to Wing Lee's. Be right back."

"No you don't, Abby," Potsie said. She slid off the bed. "If your mother opens the door and catches me in here with that dog . . ."

Abby looked at Super. "All right. Come with me. She's sleeping like a baby."

Together they hurried down the stairs and crossed

the street to the Chinese restaurant. There was a line in front of them. Abby glanced across the street at her apartment window. "I hope that dog sleeps for a long time," she said. "I hope she doesn't start to howl or something."

"Don't think about it," Potsie advised. "Think about the case instead. Think about Loretta P. Sweeny."

"And Cindy. Going to be killed tomorrow. And we don't have one decent clue to save her."

In front of them, a man turned around.

Abby stared at Wing Lee's gray tiled floor until the man turned around again. "Hey," she whispered to Potsie. "I just thought of something. I read it in Garcia's book. It's called surveillance."

"What's that?"

"Watching someone. You know. In case something happens. We'll be right there to . . ." Abby stopped when she saw the look on Potsie's face. "Anyway, that's what we'll do to Cindy. Stick to her like a fly on a Life Saver." Abby grinned. "Save her life," she couldn't resist adding.

Potsie nodded slowly. "I just hope we can save our own."

DATE: Fri. July 3.
TIME: Bedtime.

Dictionary terrible. No junonia.

HAVE TO FOLLOW CINDY AROUND. PROTECT.
<u>TOMORROW</u> <u>IS</u> <u>THE</u> <u>DAY</u>.

CHAPTER 15

Two huge brown eyes were staring at her. Abby couldn't move. She could hardly breathe.

Super.

"Get off me," she whispered, and gave the dog a little push.

Quickly she swung her legs over the side of the bed and reached for a pair of shorts. She'd have to get Super out of here as fast as she could.

She opened her bedroom door a crack and looked down the hall. In the kitchen, her father was chopping chicken livers. "How about some breakfast?" he called.

"I'm not really hungry," she said, and looked over her shoulder. Super was curled up on the bottom of the bed, eyes closed. Abby pulled the door shut behind her, wondering how she was ever going to get Super down the hall and out the front door.

In the kitchen, she leaned against the counter and

poured a glass of grape juice. "I can't stand the smell of that chicken stuff."

"Foolish child," her father said. "We can't have a picnic without chicken livers."

"Disgusting," Dan said, and sneezed. "My allergies are terrible today."

Abby reached for a piece of toast. "Probably your imagination."

He glared at her. "It was probably because some dog was hanging around the building yesterday. Pushed right past me when I opened the door. I sneezed about forty times."

Abby looked down at her plate. So that's how Super had gotten into the apartment house yesterday.

At that moment, someone pounded on the door.

They both raced for it.

Abby got there first. She turned with her hand on the doorknob. "Listen, Dan," she whispered. "I've got to warn you. Even though you're a rotten fink, you're still my brother."

"Open the door, will you?"

"Loretta P. Sweeny is a killer," she said.

"Loretta P. Who?" he asked, and closed his hand over hers on the knob.

"Ow," she said.

"Just trying to open the door."

"Stop fighting," her mother called from the kitchen.

"It's me," Potsie said from outside.

Abby opened the door.

Dan sneezed twice and headed for his bedroom.

Potsie was wearing blue shorts and a red-and-white striped shirt.

"You look like Fourth of July," Abby said. "A little conspicuous, though, for surveillance."

"You had to wear your I SOLVE CRIME shirt, I see," Potsie said, and broke off. "Dan's catching cold?"

Abby raised her eyebrows. "Allergies," she whispered. She went back into the kitchen and grabbed her toast. "We're going to the beach, Mom."

Her mother pushed at her hair. "Whew, it's hot. We'll be there in a little while. Look for us. We'll sit near the water in front of the Little Theater."

Abby nodded and went back to her bedroom with Potsie. She handed Super the toast. She took it in one gulp, then yawned and scratched at one ear with her back leg.

The whole bed shook.

"Stop that noise," Dan shouted from his bedroom. "I can't even hear my radio."

Abby picked up the shells and put them carefully in her knapsack. "Maybe we can sell these" — she crossed her fingers — "after the mystery is solved."

"I hope," Potsie said.

Abby went to her dresser and took the wallet out from under a jumble of underwear. "We may need this for evidence." She looked around. "I think we're ready. Now how are we going to get Super out?" she asked. "Down the fire escape?"

"Down the hall when nobody's looking?" Potsie asked at the same time.

Abby shoved the screen up and climbed out on the fire escape. "Here, Super," she called softly.

Slowly Super slid off the bed and padded over to the window.

Potsie tugged at her and patted the sill. "Climb up," she said.

Super yawned again and dug her nails into the rug.

Potsie pushed harder. "It's no good," she said, red-faced, after a few minutes.

Abby climbed back into the room and opened the door a little. The bathroom door was closed and she could hear her mother running water for a bath. Her father was nowhere in sight.

"Let's go," she said, and rushed down the hall.

In his bedroom, Dan sneezed again.

"God bless you," Potsie muttered as they dashed out the door and closed it behind them.

Twenty minutes later, perspiration streaming down their faces, they reached the beach. "Bumper car place first," Abby said.

They hurried down the street and peered over the low wooden fence. There was a long line at the ticket counter, and cars were whizzing around the track.

"Hard to tell . . ." Abby began, standing on tiptoes.

Potsie clutched her arm hard. "Look, Abby," she said, and pointed.

Across the street, heading for the boardwalk, was a skinny girl with long dark hair streaming out behind her. She was moving fast, practically running, and she was holding up a red skirt with one hand.

"The mummy," Potsie breathed.

Abby felt a chill ripple down her back. "Loretta P. Sweeny."

They stared at each other for a moment.

"What'll we do?" Abby asked.

"Get out of here." Potsie took a step backward. "Fast."

Abby looked after the girl as she started up the ramp and disappeared behind a group of people carrying a beach umbrella. "Forget about Cindy," Abby said.

"You don't care if she gets killed?"

Abby waved her hand impatiently. "Come on, Pots. Before we lose Loretta P. Sweeny. Don't you see? We'll follow her instead. Stay with her all day. We'll be there when she tries to . . ."

Potsie took another step back. "You said we were going to watch Cindy. Not Loretta. Not the killer."

Abby looked up toward the boardwalk. "Please, Pots, hurry."

Then, as Potsie stood there, still shaking her head, Abby raced toward the boardwalk. "I'm going after her now," she yelled. "Before it's too late."

CHAPTER 16

Breathless, Abby sprinted up the ramp, darted around the people with the umbrella, and came to a dead stop when she hit the boardwalk.

Loretta P. Sweeny was right in front of her.

In back of her, Potsie was screaming, "Wait up. I can't go so fast." She bumped into Abby. Super skidded to a stop and began to lick Abby's ankle.

"Stop," she whispered, and wiggled her leg. "She's going to see us."

But Loretta didn't seem to notice them. She was standing in front of the souvenir stand. "Have you seen Dan?" she asked the man.

"Should be here any minute," the man said. "I'll tell him you were looking for him."

"Remind him about the junonia, will you?" she said. "I've got to have one in" — she looked at her watch —"an hour or two. I'm depending on it.

I don't know what I'll do if . . ." She stopped talking and started across the boardwalk for the Little Theater.

Abby grabbed Potsie's shoulder. "Junonia," she whispered.

They watched as Loretta stopped and looked into the big glass doors of the theater, then shoved the door open and disappeared inside.

Abby went over to the souvenir stand. The man was talking to a woman in a pink bathing suit. "Mister?" Abby asked.

The man turned his head.

"Sorry. I just want to ask you about a junonia."

The man grinned. "You're the second one who asked for that." He scratched at a peel on his nose. "Dan, the kid who works here, is trying to find one. Stop back later."

Abby leaned forward. "But what is . . ."

The souvenir man didn't hear her. He had gone into the back of the stand to get something for the woman in the bathing suit.

"Come on, Pots," she said. "We'll see about that in a little while. Right now, we don't want to lose Loretta."

They walked over to the theater and peered through the glass doors.

Loretta P. Sweeny was nowhere in sight.

A boy was sweeping the lobby. He waved his hand at them. "The show's not until tonight," he said, and pointed to a green and white sign on the wall.

<u>Big Performance</u>
July Fourth
See:

<u>IF</u> THE <u>SHOE</u> <u>FITS</u>

by
Loretta P. Sweeny
Starring
Kevin Delio
and
Holly Monk
Sets by Kiki Krumback

"Wouldn't you know," Abby said, "Dan's friends. They're always into everything."

For a moment, they watched as the boy finished sweeping the lobby, rested his broom against the wall, and pushed the doors open. "Can't come in," he said as he headed for the hot dog stand.

As soon as his back was turned, Abby pulled open the doors and held them for Potsie and Super.

They tiptoed into the lobby. Abby motioned to the stairs off to one side. "The balcony," she whispered. "We'll be able to see the whole theater. Find out where Loretta is."

With hardly a sound, they raced up the blue-carpeted steps.

Abby turned.

Super was standing on the bottom step, wagging her tail a little, and whining softly.

"Darn dog," she whispered. "Come on." She raced back down again, grabbed Super's collar, and gave a little tug. Slowly Super lumbered up the stairs.

A moment later, they pulled open the door to the balcony. It was dark inside, and cool.

Abby got down on her hands and knees, opened the door a little more, and ducked behind the last row of seats.

"We'll just stay here a little while," Abby said as Potsie and Super crawled in next to her. "See what's going on." She grabbed Super's collar as the dog began to chew on the edge of the seat.

A moment later, they heard Loretta's voice. "Is someone in here?" she said.

At the same moment, the balcony door clicked shut behind them. Slowly Abby reached out and turned the knob.

"Locked," she whispered. "Potsie, we're locked in."

"Locked in with a killer." Potsie's lips trembled.

"Who's that?" Loretta yelled.

Slowly Abby raised her head over the row of seats, but she couldn't see anyone. "She must be downstairs somewhere," she whispered, barely moving her lips.

Abby looked around wildly. Behind her, up high, was a small window. The panes were painted black. If she could just get up there and pry it open, maybe they could get out, or at least yell for help.

Still on her hands and knees, she inched her way toward the window. She stood up slowly, trying not to make a sound.

She pushed at the window with her fingertips.

It slid open easily, letting in air and sunlight and the sound of the crowd of people on the beach. She ducked down.

From below, there was no noise. Either Loretta was

under the balcony where she couldn't see the light, or she was climbing the stairs toward them.

"Give me a boost," Abby whispered frantically.

Potsie held out her hands and grabbed Abby's foot.

Abby reached up, grabbed the sill, and slid over. The window was small, so small that it seemed to take forever for her to pull herself through.

She looked out. A roof, flat and full of gravel. And next to it, the roof of the souvenir stand.

She scrambled to the edge. Down below, near the water, she could see her father setting up their old green umbrella, and in front, the boardwalk was crowded with people. Dan was blowing up an alligator balloon for a little girl.

"Dan," she yelled. "Help. Someone. Please."

No one looked up. No one even heard her. A million people were screaming, the water was rushing back and forth, and the merry-go-round was blaring.

She turned back. She could see Potsie's fingers trying to grip the window ledge. "Come on, Pots," she said urgently.

But she knew there was no way that Potsie could get out without someone to give her a boost. The window was just up too high.

CHAPTER 17

Use your head, she told herself. She had read that in Garcia's book about forty times.

She raised her voice. "Listen, Potsie. Hold still so you can hear me."

From inside there was silence.

"Pots?"

"What?"

"Take Super's collar off. And your belt. Tie them together. Pots? Are you listening?"

"Tie them together," Potsie repeated.

"Yes. Knot one end to the doorknob and the other to one of the seats. Then Loretta won't be able to open the door."

"All right." Potsie's voice came back faintly. "I will."

"I'm going to get help," Abby said. "Somehow."

She looked around wondering if there was a way down from the outside. Maybe next door, from the souvenir man's roof. She'd have to go as fast as she could. A collar and a little string belt wouldn't keep

Loretta P. Sweeny out for more than a couple of seconds.

She hurried toward the souvenir man's roof, feeling the gravel sliding under her feet.

She jumped down onto it, twisting her ankle a little. But she didn't stop to rub it or to catch her breath. She spotted a ladder at the back end.

It was just a bunch of rungs strung together, old and rusted, but it was bolted to the back wall. She rested her weight against it. It felt strong and solid.

She let herself down. Then limping, she hurried around the back of the souvenir stand and through the alley toward the front of the boardwalk.

Loretta P. Sweeny was just disappearing into the fortune-teller's booth.

Abby collapsed against the edge of the souvenir stand and rubbed at her ankle. Potsie and Super were safe.

She thought about going around to the theater to tell Potsie. She wondered how long Loretta would stay in the booth. Maybe she should wait and see. She looked back and forth trying to make up her mind.

Someone grabbed her arm.

She looked up. It was the lady whose friend had been kidnapped. Mildred Pane.

"Are you Abby?" she asked. "Dan's sister?"

Abby nodded. "How did you know?"

"Dan told me you were wearing a shirt that said I SOLVE CRIME. He said you wanted to be a detective."

Abby nodded again, still trying to catch her breath.

"He said you're pretty good at it."

"He did?" Abby said, a nice feeling spreading through her. She'd never figure Dan out. She looked around. "Where is he anyway?"

"Not here now. He's taking one last look for a junonia. He's got two customers who . . ." Mildred bit her lip. "But that's not my problem. My problem is Mrs. Upernicki."

"Your friend?" Abby asked. "The one who's been kidnapped?"

"Kidnapped? You think she's been kidnapped?" Mildred closed her eyes. "I never thought of that. Mrs. Upernicki has a strange habit of wandering around. She doesn't pay attention to what she's doing and then she gets herself into all kinds of messes." Mildred wiped at her eyes. "Anyway, I just told Dan I was looking for Mrs. Upernicki. He said to ask you to look around. . . ." Her voice trailed off.

Abby put her hand out. "I will, really. I just have to get my friend. She's locked in the theater."

"How . . ."

"A mistake," Abby mumbled.

"All right, dear. I'll be walking along the boardwalk. Maybe someone's seen . . ."

"I'll be right back," Abby called over her shoulder. "Hey, by the way, do you know what a junonia is?"

Mildred nodded. "I certainly do," she called. "Tan . . ."

Abby bumped into a teenage boy who was weaving back and forth on a skateboard. She turned back. "What did you say?" she called.

Mildred waved. "Like Mrs. Upernicki's hair," she called back.

Abby sighed. She looked at the fortune-teller's booth. Loretta P. Sweeny was still inside. She'd have to go for Potsie. Charge right down there, get back before Loretta came out.

She raced into the lobby of the Little Theater.

The boy was standing at the back end. "You can't come in," he said. "Come tonight. It's a fairy tale with a twist."

"Got to get my friend," Abby gasped. She dashed around him and up the stairs.

"I've got a gun," Potsie yelled from behind the door. "And a dog with rabies."

Abby pounded on the door. "It's me, your old friend."

Inside, Potsie was shouting. "Get away. I'm going to . . ."

Abby turned the knob and pulled hard. The door banged open. Super's collar and Potsie's belt flew across the seats.

Potsie threw her arms around Abby. "Saved," she said. "Thank goodness."

"Hurry," Abby said. "Loretta's in the fortune-teller's booth. We can't lose her now."

Potsie stood up. "We have to get out of here anyway. Super's chewed a hole in the rug."

Abby raced down the aisle and scooped up Super's collar. Then she stooped to buckle it on the dog before they dashed for the stairs and outside.

In front of the theater, they stopped to catch their breath. "There goes Cindy," Potsie said, pointing.

Abby glanced at the beach. Cindy, in a black polka-dot bathing suit and heart-shaped glasses, was heading for the sand. And Dan was just coming up the ramp with a pile of shells in his hands.

As he passed, Abby grabbed him by the arm. "You said you didn't know Loretta P. Sweeny. That murderer. You'd better tell me right away. What's going on?"

Dan raised his shoulders. "I know all the girls," he said, grinning. "But not anyone named Loretta . . ."

"Long hair," Abby said. "Brown. Brown eyes. Braces. Lots of silvery braces."

"Oh," Dan said, "that's . . ." He broke off. "Hey, you found . . ."

At that moment, Loretta P. Sweeny came charging out of the fortune-teller's booth.

"Sister Amelia should be back any minute," she yelled at Dan. "Did you get the junonia?"

"Sorry, no," Dan yelled back.

Loretta raced down the ramp and started across the sand. She was going so fast that the sand sprayed up behind her.

"Come on," Abby yelled to Potsie. "After her. This is it. She's on her way to kill Cindy." She yanked off her sneakers so she could run faster.

"Wait a minute," Dan said.

"See you later," Abby yelled. "We've got to stop the killer."

CHAPTER 18

The sand was hot. Burning. Abby raced across it, wishing she were still wearing sneakers. She thought of tonight's play. *If the Shoe Fits.* If only she had flip-flops on, or something.

Loretta P. Sweeny was halfway across the beach already, way ahead of her. And Cindy was kneeling at the edge of the water. She didn't even see Loretta coming.

Abby glanced over her shoulder. Potsie was just coming down the ramp.

At the water's edge, there was nobody under her family's old green umbrella. Her mother and father must be in the water.

But Super was right with her, racing along, barking in short little yelps. She thought they were playing some kind of game. She kept circling in front of Abby, slowing her down.

"Watch where you're going," someone yelled. "You're getting sand all over the place."

Abby veered away. She fell over a man who was reading a book.

"Hard to get any peace around here," the man complained.

"Sorry." Abby picked up the book and handed it to him.

She pulled herself to her feet. Cindy was still kneeling at the water's edge. Loretta P. Sweeny had stopped running, though. She was bending over, a few feet away from Cindy, looking at the sand.

Abby raced toward her, then reached out and caught her by the shoulder.

Loretta spun around. "Thief," she yelled when she saw Abby.

"Murderer," Abby yelled back.

"Out of my way," Loretta said. "You took the last junonia on the whole beach and if Sister Amelia finds out that Cynthia broke hers, we're going to get skinned alive."

Potsie slid to a stop in front of them and Super began to chew on her toe.

"What's going on?" Potsie asked. "Did you warn Cindy?"

But Cynthia was coming toward them. "Sorry, Rita," she called to Loretta P. Sweeny. "I'm still looking, but I can't find a junonia."

"Rita?" Abby repeated. "Loretta P. Sweeny is Rita?"

"Watch out, Cindy," Potsie yelled. "She's going to kill you."

Super began to bark.

Abby sank down on the sand. "I don't believe it," she muttered. "Loretta P. Sweeny is Princess Rita Rose."

Just then Dan went by. He had a case over his shoulder. "Souvenirs," he was yelling. "Special for July Fourth."

He stopped when he saw them. "Hi, everybody." He shifted the case to his other shoulder. "All set for the play tonight, Rita? Cinderella, isn't it?"

"Cinderella?" Potsie asked. "I thought it was something about a shoe."

"There's a shoe in Cinderella," Abby said. "And the boy who was sweeping out the theater said the play was a fairy tale with a twist."

Dan started across the sand, then looked back. "Hey, I didn't know you knew each other."

"All I know is that one has a disease," Cindy called after him. "And the other one is crazy."

Dan started to laugh. "They're both crazy."

"The one who's crazy," Abby yelled after him, "is my brother Dan, the souvenir king."

Rita started to laugh. "You're Dan's sister? The one who wants to be a detective?"

"And you're Princess Rita Rose? Or is it Loretta P. Sweeny?"

"Same person," Princess Rita Rose said. "Loretta P. Sweeny is my writing name."

"What is everybody talking about?" Potsie asked.

Abby turned toward her. "Don't you see, Pots?" she asked patiently. "Princess Rita Rose is Loretta P. Sweeny. She wrote *If the Shoe Fits*. It's about Cinderella."

Princess Rita Rose nodded absently. She was still looking around on the sand. "Modern-day. Cindy. Not Cinderella. No glass slippers. Wedgies. I killed her off. Let the half sister get the prince for a change."

"Good grief," Abby said. "I just realized. Cindy. Cinderella. P for prince."

Potsie gasped. "So that's what the note in the wallet was."

"Wallet?" Princess Rita Rose asked. "You found my wallet?"

Abby nodded. "We've been trying to find out who owns it all week."

"Didn't even have time to swim," Potsie said.

"Wallet's probably full of germs," Cindy said.

"I really don't have a disease," Potsie said. "It was just a . . ."

"Just a joke," Abby said.

"Not very nice," Cindy said.

Abby sighed. "Sorry. I'd try to explain, but it's just too complicated." She looked at Princess Rita Rose. "Hey. You told my fortune in the rain."

Rita shook her head. "No, that was Cindy. She took my place all week so I could write. Threw red ribbons on the floor for blood. Said crazy things. She was terrific." Rita sighed. "If only she hadn't dropped Sister Amelia's junonia."

"What's that?" Potsie asked.

"Another thing I've been trying to find out," Abby said.

"A shell," Princess Rita Rose said. "Didn't you know that? Long. Tan and brown."

"Like Mrs. Upernicki's hair," Abby said absently.

"My grandmother, Sister Amelia, says it's her good luck charm. She always kept it in a jar. She thinks it helps her tell fortunes. But now . . ."

"It's in pieces." Abby nodded, remembering the night she had sneaked into the fortune-teller's booth.

"I nearly had a junonia to replace it," Rita said. "It was almost in my hand." She pointed to Abby. "Then you grabbed it. Stole . . ."

"Stole?" Abby repeated. "I never . . ."

"It was right on top of the castle. I reached for it and . . ."

"That was you?" Abby said. "You stole the shells out of my knapsack anyway."

"I did," Cindy said. "They were junk, all broken. I threw them away for you."

"We still have that shell," Potsie said. "Long and tan. It's in Abby's knapsack."

"Would you . . ." Rita began. "Do you think you could . . ."

"Sell it?" Abby asked, grinning. "Why not? We're in the shell business."

"Thank goodness." Rita grinned back. "How about some free tickets to a terrific play?"

Abby nodded. "Sure. Come on. Let's get my knapsack."

She stood up. "Mystery's all over," she said to Potsie, and started toward the boardwalk.

At the same moment, someone at the water's edge began to yell.

CHAPTER 19

"Good grief," Abby said. "What now?" She stopped to look back across the sand.

"Super, I'll bet," Potsie said. "Into something else."

"Go ahead," Abby told her. "Get Rita's wallet for her. And the junonia. I'll go back and see what's going on."

She headed toward the water. Out of the corner of her eye, she could see her mother and father standing next to their umbrella. Her father was drying his shoulders with a green beach towel.

In front of her, two little boys were pointing. One of them was crying.

Abby shaded her eyes and looked out at the water.

Super. Of course. She was swimming around with a rope in her mouth. At the end of the rope was a little blue and white raft.

"Super," Abby yelled. "Bring that back."

The little boy pulled at her hand. "That dog took

my raft. It's going to be gone in a minute. Out in the ocean."

"Don't worry," she said, "I'll get it somehow."

"You're not supposed to have a dog here," the other boy said. "You're going to get in trouble."

Abby sighed. She took a few steps into the water. "Do me a favor," she asked a girl who was standing nearby. "Get my dog?"

"Suppose he bites," the girl said. "Better get him yourself."

Abby waded in a little farther. The water was icy cold. It felt wonderful on her legs. "Here, Super," she called. "Come on, girl."

Super kept swimming around in circles just out of reach.

Abby looked back. Her father was standing at the edge of the water now, the towel draped around his neck. He smiled at Abby. "Go ahead," he said. "Let me see you swim."

She shook her head. "You know I can't. I'm trying to get that raft."

"You can do it," her father said.

"Dad, how about you?" she pleaded.

The little boy started to yell again. "Get my raft, hurry."

Her father smiled again. "Go ahead, Abby."

She took another step. She could feel the water on her knees, and then on her waist, as she kept going.

She leaned forward and sliced her arms through the water. Then, carefully she raised one foot up and kicked. A little water went in her mouth. It was salty, but not really scary.

Gingerly she raised the other foot and kicked once. And then again. She could feel her body moving. Swimming. Two strokes. Then three.

She grabbed the raft with one hand and Super's tan hair with the other.

"I swam," she yelled to her father. "I did it."

"I knew you could," he yelled back.

Holding on to Super, she let herself be dragged into the shallow water.

They waded out of the water and across the sand. One of the little boys grabbed the raft.

Wait till Potsie heard she was swimming.

Super shook herself, pelting Abby with drops of water.

From across the sand, someone was calling.

Abby looked across the sand. It was Mildred Pane. She was holding out her arms. "Mrs. Upernicki," she shouted.

Super took off. She pounded over the sand, dashed between the two boys and the raft, and jumped up to lick Mildred's face.

"What a detective," Mildred yelled to Abby. "You found Mrs. Upernicki."

DATE: July 4.
TIME: Late . . . after the play . . . after the fireworks.

CRIME SOLVED.

Mrs. Upernicki's collar was worn. Only part of
the name was left:

MRS. UPERNICKI
S UPER

Tomorrow:
Have to find new crime. Dan says try the post office.
Lots of Wanted posters on the wall.

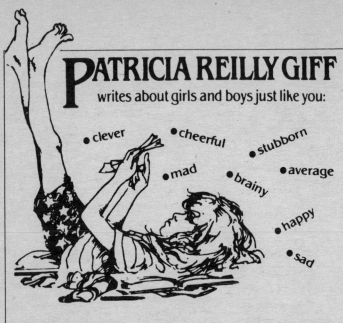

Beverly Cleary